DALLAS

BROTHERHOOD PROTECTORS WORLD

REGAN BLACK

Twisted Page Press LLC

BROTHERHOOD PROTECTORS

ORIGINAL SERIES BY ELLE JAMES

Brotherhood Protectors Series

With special thanks to Elle James for inviting me into her world of Brotherhood Protectors.

GUARDIAN AGENCY: DALLAS

ABOUT *GUARDIAN AGENCY: DALLAS*

When hope is lost, truth is blurred, and your life is on the line,
it's time to call in the Guardian Agency.

Running for her life...

When a typical day at her cafe in Eagle Rock was interrupted by a young woman desperate to escape her captors, Marnie Kemper gladly intervened. She also gladly agreed to testify against the men involved. Now, days before the start of the trial, her security detail is killed and she's alone, terrified, and unsure who to trust.

A stunning stranger is her only hope.

Dallas Winston's Army career ended abruptly when he and his K9 partner were shot during a drug bust.

Thankfully, the Guardian Agency gave him a second chance at a meaningful career. When he gets the order to rescue a witness and salvage a high-profile case, he follows procedure and rushes in.

Soon it's clear that standard tactics won't be enough to keep Marnie alive. Forced to get creative, Dallas must lower his defenses to earn Marnie's trust as they navigate a deadly web of corruption.

Visit ReganBlack.com for a full list of titles, excerpts and upcoming release dates.
For early access to new releases, exclusive prizes, and much more,
subscribe to Regan's monthly newsletter.

CHAPTER 1

LEAVING THE BED AND BREAKFAST, Dallas Winston walked the tidy streets of Eagle Rock, Montana toward the Blue Moose Tavern to meet up with his friend Joseph Kuntz. Kujo had hit the jackpot landing here. Driving in yesterday, Dallas had been awed by the rugged beauty of the Crazy Mountains framing the landscape. Cattle ranches stretched out like a patchwork quilt. According to Kujo, some ranches remained serious operations and others were sprawling getaways for wealthy people and celebrities willing to pay big for seclusion and privacy.

Plenty of that to be had here.

He pulled out his cell phone and took a couple of pictures, texting them to his technical support and research assistant, Tyler. He followed the text with a quick message: Taking a few days but ready for anything.

A few days on the moon? Tyler replied.

Tyler never ran out of snark, but he was damn good at his job and they made a good team, without ever meeting face to face.

Dallas looked to the mountains. Yeah, on a map, Eagle Rock might get overlooked, too remote to bother. In person, it was clear this little corner of the world offered a great deal. The town boasted every convenience and amenity in addition to the good kind of small-town charm. Amazing what could happen when a community cared. Of course, a boost of star-power like Sadie McClain, the Hollywood darling who married Kujo's boss Hank Patterson, sure didn't hurt.

Still, this place gave the impression that the wild-west could make a glorious comeback any minute. Dallas wasn't here to play cowboy or escape a flock of paparazzi. He was here for a little diversion until the Guardian Agency assigned him his next protection order. Eagle Rock was perched at the edge of his designated territory. Unless he was off the roster, the agency expected him to be able to respond swiftly to any crisis in his region. He had a go-bag in his truck at all times, but he was hoping for an uninterrupted week to relax.

Maybe it was the endless sky, clean air, or just the sheer distance from his troubles, but Dallas already felt a sense of relief here. The constant knots in his shoulders eased a bit. Even the spike of pain in his hip that followed him everywhere was easier to ignore out here.

Good for Kujo. The man deserved some peace and quiet after his intense years of military service. Dallas was looking forward to catching up with his friend and meeting Six, the K9 partner Kujo rescued when they'd both been declared unfit for duty.

As military K9 handlers, Dallas and Kujo had met years ago during an annual refresher course. Dallas's service with the Army Military Police kept him state-side while Kujo and his K9s had been on countless ops on the other side of the world. Handlers were a tight-knit community within the military and Dallas had heard about it when Kujo adopted Six. He admired his friend's ability to make that decision, but Dallas wasn't ready. Not even close. He mentally crossed his fingers that Kujo wouldn't suggest adopting a dog.

Pausing across the street from the tavern, Dallas pushed his sunglasses to the top of his head. Neon signs in the front windows advertised beer and pool tables. Anticipation smothered any worry about dog talk. Clearly Kujo had forgotten that Dallas had honed his pool-hustling skills during his early Army days.

He walked inside and spotted Kujo immediately. His friend waved him over to a high top near a pool table and introduced Dallas to the others, all former military men. Putting names with faces, he shook hands with Duke, a man who matched Kujo in size, Taz, who had a slightly leaner build, and Hank Patterson, founder of the Brotherhood Protectors.

The guys were friendly and Dallas appreciated the

immediate camaraderie. Working with the Guardian Agency, he was usually on his own, with only the support of a technical assistant on the other end of the phone. The solo assignments were best for him, he wasn't ready to worry about the safety of anyone but the client, but he could see the appeal of Patterson's setup.

Kujo ordered another round for everyone while Taz racked the balls for the next game, inviting Dallas to break. Chalking the cue stick, he lined up his preferred opening shot and bent forward. The movement caused the damned nerve in his leg to gripe. He waited that out and made an excellent opening break, only to feel his phone vibrating in his hip pocket.

"Hang on." He had to check if it was business. Rule number one for Guardian Agency bodyguards was never keep a client waiting. A motto he took seriously and a philosophy that bolstered his battered pride after his medical discharge from the Army.

Looking at his phone, he saw the single word: PROTECT Details would come through within minutes and he had to be ready to move.

"Sorry, guys." He tucked the cue stick back in the rack on the wall. "Duty calls. It was great to meet you all." He shook hands with the others and promised to try and visit after this case. On his way out, he stopped at the bar and dropped some cash to cover the next round.

Outside, he regretted walking over as his leg fought

the quick pace back to the bed and breakfast. By the time he'd checked out and climbed into his truck, the name and location for his assignment hit his phone. Female. Marnie Kemper. Currently located at the Federal courthouse in Helena, Montana.

"Hang on, Marnie," he muttered as he hit the highway and turned west. "Help is on the way."

CHAPTER 2

HUDDLED in the dark closet of a low-end motel, Marnie Kemper was sure of only one thing: she had to save herself. This hiding place wouldn't shelter her indefinitely. She'd been lucky the room hadn't been rented today.

Her stomach rumbled, reminding her that she hadn't eaten since breakfast. Her protective detail had been escorting her to lunch when her world had shattered at the side door of the courthouse. She pressed the heels of her hands to her eyes to stem the flow of more useless tears.

Just this morning, in an upscale hotel room near the airport with comprehensive security systems, she'd convinced herself that life would return to normal someday soon. After months of protective custody, she'd started counting down the days until she'd be home in Eagle Rock, sleeping in her own bed, waking early to walk to her café to prep for the morning rush.

While dressing for the meeting this morning with the U.S. Attorney's office, she'd replayed her small part in saving Autumn Curley, a young woman who'd been kidnapped from the Crow Indian Reservation over a year ago. The day should've been simple, straightforward. All Marnie had to do was review her testimony and prepare for what would surely be an aggressive cross-examination by the defense team.

Just this morning, she'd been confident about this final phase of the judicial process. Once she gave her testimony she could get back to her routine, back to the frequent compliments that her mashed potatoes were too smooth and creamy to be the real deal. She could hardly wait until her biggest concern was the price of beef.

Marnie hadn't ever been truly worried about the trial. The defense had a client to protect, but no matter what they tried, she wouldn't let them twist her words. She had crystal-clear recollection of that day and she knew she could relay the horrible events effectively to the jury.

Now, she might never get the chance to testify. A scream built in her throat and she covered her mouth with her hands. One stray whimper could be the death of her. She wouldn't go out on a damned whimper. She *would* make a plan and get herself out of here.

Someone had shot Jerry Calvin, lead of her protective detail, as the two of them had exited the courthouse in Helena. Another scream clawed for release. She had to hold her breath to keep it in as she recalled the bullet plowing into his chest. A bullet meant for her? Must have been. It had struck him because he'd shoved her to her knees, out of the way.

Then he'd pressed his car keys into her hand and told her to run. Were those words his last?

She hoped not. Closing her eyes tight, she prayed that he'd survived. Jerry had shared stories about his wife and young daughters, his parents down in Texas, and their big family summer vacation plans.

Marnie rolled the closet door back just enough to see how much light remained outside. The bright daylight pouring through the window threw her off. She hadn't worn a watch in years and this was the first time she missed it. Although in her heart it felt like she'd been tucked into the closet for days, clearly it had only been a few hours at best.

When no one stormed into the room, she peeked out of the closet far enough to spot the digital clock near the bed, confirming that it was late afternoon. Just over three hours in hiding.

When to bolt? How?

She tucked herself back into the shadows as shock dragged her mind through the chaos once again. At the courthouse, with Jerry's words ringing in her ears and his blood sticky on her hands, getting to his car had been a blur of color and terror. It was a miracle she hadn't hurt someone in her mad rush to distance herself from the gunfire. Afraid the car could be followed she'd dumped it at a strip mall and made her way through an arts and crafts store to the bathroom. She'd washed the blood from her hands and tried to think, tried to put the pieces in order.

In that bathroom, her first instinct had been to call the café, to ask someone there to come get her. No purse, no phone. Most likely her purse was at the courthouse, somewhere near Jerry, lost when he saved her life. She was probably better off without it, since her cell phone and credit cards could be traced. Still, the emergency twenty dollars hidden in her bra, a habit from her college days, wouldn't go far.

Uncertain how to ask for help without gaining too much attention, she'd waited near the restroom, meandering through the aisles near the back of the store until an employee opened the rear door, then she'd slipped outside. The late-spring weather was too balmy, the day too bright and clean and happy for the darkness assaulting her mind. Every sound gave her a start, every person became a threat. No one had prepared her for this. She was too scared to call the police, didn't trust them to keep her safe. During her time at the safe house, she'd frequently heard her protective detail talk about the long reach of the criminals she would testify against.

She'd scurried along in the shadows of passersby,

wondering where to hide until she noticed the motel. Several doors were open as housekeeping cleaned the rooms. She made her move, sneaking into a room while the maid was distracted.

But now what? It didn't feel safe to move yet, but she couldn't wait here for the inevitable.

Six months after helping a young woman escape, Marnie was the one in need of an assist. Who could she reach out to without making things worse? Bad people with deep pockets and a long reach wanted her dead. Anyone she called would join her in the cross-hairs of a killer.

Marnie couldn't help wondering about Autumn. Had her protection been compromised too? If so, Marnie *had* to live. She could not let these evil, creepy bastards win.

Determined to come up with a workable escape plan, she held her breath, listening. Thin walls were one benefit of a cheap motel. No voices outside. She crawled out of the closet, staying low as she crept to the closet. Keeping as far away from the window as possible, she reached up and slid the chain into place, turning the deadbolt as quietly as possible.

Breathing easier, she crossed the room on her hands and knees, under the open window. Pulling the curtains closed could alert the motel staff and she didn't harbor any illusions that the bad guys had given up. Her movements to and from the courthouse had been a secret. Someone had leaked the information.

She peeked outside again, her gaze going to the mountains in the distance. She knew that national forest and recreational area inside and out. Her odds of surviving out there were probably a hundred times better than waiting for a killer to find her here.

She just had to get from here to there in one piece.

DALLAS USED the hands-free button on the steering wheel to answer the incoming call from Tyler. Per Guardian Agency protocol, they'd never met in person, but the man was rock-steady in a crisis and able to gather reliable intel before Dallas could type a query into his Google search bar.

"Still tense here at the courthouse," he said in lieu of a greeting. "Tell me you have something helpful."

"Don't I always? Your client of record is U.S. Attorney, Billie Hamilton," Tyler continued without waiting for a reply. "That's privileged info, by the way. The protect order is for a star witness in the upcoming case against those bastards who were caught trafficking Native American women."

Dallas ignored the flare of anger, stretching his jaw to avoid grinding his teeth. So many crimes against women went unreported and it was exponentially worse among Native Americans. Proud of his Blackfeet heritage, the outrage at crimes against his ancestors, recent and long gone, had remained on a perpetual simmer in his blood for most of his life.

"I don't suppose our client informed Marnie Kemper of my arrival?" He'd circled the area several times and was now following the latest navigation prompts Tyler had sent.

A low whistle came through the speakers. "Not a chance. The lead on her protective detail was shot and killed as they left the courthouse late this morning. From what I can piece together, she took his car, disappeared and hasn't popped back on the radar."

Dallas could tell by the sound of a rattling keyboard that Tyler was working at warp speed to find the missing witness. "So where the hell are you sending me?"

"The safe house," Tyler replied absently. "It's the last known address I have for her. Where else would she go?"

That was the question. Dallas turned into a residential neighborhood, bumping up against heavy police presence immediately. He was directed away from the safe house location and the navigation immediately tried to reroute him. Muting the guide on the app, he said, "Cops have the safe house surrounded. If she's in there, I can't be."

"If she was there, your protect order would be revoked," Tyler pointed out.

Dallas sighed and wound his way back out of the

neighborhood. "Where did she dump the car? What else do we have?"

Tyler swore. "Nothing that qualifies as helpful."

"Tell me anyway. Walk me through it one more time."

Dallas listened to Tyler's recitation starting with the time of the shooting at the courthouse and the resulting actions. Marnie had taken the car and left the area well before it had been cordoned off as a crime scene. Her purse had been found near the body of the victim and eventually police located the car near a strip mall.

"Why not drive straight out of town?" Dallas queried. "Or to the police station. Back to safety." He couldn't make sense of the woman's decisions.

"All good questions." Tyler whistled low and then swore again. "I got into the cameras at the safe house," he said. "No sign of her in that area since they left this morning. Good thing too."

"Why?"

"Because someone else was watching the place. Male, lean build, bald. Wearing a dark suit, but he doesn't look like FBI to me."

What kind of killer would be careless enough to get caught on camera? A killer without fear of consequences. Dallas suppressed a surge of vengeful anticipation. "Is he still there?" He'd park and go in on foot if necessary.

"No." Tyler muttered obscenities. "Looks like he got a call and left the area."

Dallas aimed toward the strip mall where Kemper had left the car. "Kemper owned a café in Eagle Rock, right?"

"She's still the owner of record," Tyler confirmed.

It was a glimmer of a silver lining. "Coordinate with Hank Patterson's Brotherhood Protectors to keep an eye out at the café and her house."

"You think she'll go home?"

Dallas took a deep breath. He didn't know enough about her to anticipate her next move. He parked across the street from the strip mall. A normal person would panic when being shot at and panic made people unpredictable. "Tell me more about her."

Tyler obliged. "Montana born and raised. Boarding school, business degree and loads of restaurant experience before she opened her café. She was taken into protective custody after helping a Native American woman escape from a trafficking ring."

Dallas had read about the Autumn Curley case at the time. An icy grip coiled around his spine. Human trafficking was evil enough without adding in the experience and baggage Dallas carried. Women were disappearing from reservations all across the west at an alarming rate. He'd answered domestic violence calls and assisted with missing person cases during his tenure with the Army on various stateside bases. If his

K9 partner hadn't been killed in action on their last call, he might still be there.

Instead he was here, working a case that cut a little too close to his soul. There would be time later to sort out if this protection order was a good challenge or just one more hurdle to overcome.

"Remind me which crime syndicate the girl escaped from."

"That seems to be a secret more closely guarded than three key witnesses," Tyler groused. "It's going to take more digging."

Tyler-code for a creative, if not strictly legal, approach to intel gathering. "Fair enough," Dallas said. "I'm at the strip mall. There's no police presence and no sign of the car she dumped."

"Seriously? They were quick to get that to the impound lot," Tyler said. "Hang on. Bingo!"

Dallas stretched his stiff leg, waiting for the good news.

"She left the strip mall through the back door of that craft store." Tyler made the noises that indicated he was following the trail from camera to camera. "Nervous as a cat," he murmured. "No clothing change or disguise." He swore. "And she disappears again about three blocks north of your location."

That was the starting point he needed. "All right, I'm moving. Thanks." He set his phone to vibrate only. "If she does reappear, let me know." He wished there was a way to tell Kemper help was close. He didn't want to scare her further.

Dallas mentally gave Kemper points for perseverance, assuming she hadn't been caught or killed in the past hour. People did strange things when they were terrified, but so far the signs indicated she'd kept her wits about her. He found a place to park near the intersection where Tyler had last seen Kemper and studied the area. A plumbing supply store occupied one large warehouse and butted up to a furniture store. Across the street a building was under construction and another block up, Dallas could see the sign for a cut-rate motel.

While he analyzed the area for potential hiding places, his mind wandered. How did the U.S. Attorney know to call the Guardian Agency? And why call in a private bodyguard, when the FBI and state law enforcement officers were equally invested in the outcome of the case? Did Hamilton suspect a leak somewhere in the long chain of due process?

The agency didn't advertise, but they had an excellent success record and a reputation for discretion. So Hamilton must have a personal connection. The identity of the agency founder was a mystery and all in-person meetings were handled by the law firm of Gamble and Swann. Maybe the world of lawyers was smaller than Dallas thought.

Didn't matter and it sure wasn't the critical point he needed to focus on. There was a woman being hunted so that others could avoid the consequences for kidnapping, trafficking, and whatever other charges the prosecution piled onto the case. Where would she hide?

Personally, he'd go off-grid. Change his clothes, ditch his wallet, credit cards and cell phone. Able to hold his own in nearly any situation, he'd hitchhike out of town. Or steal a car. Too bad there was a lack of promising truck stops or diners in the immediate vicinity.

Marnie Kemper wasn't him. According to the few details he had, she was a bit shorter than average with a light frame. Hamilton was lucky she wasn't already a statistic. His role was to safely recover her and keep her hidden until she could testify. He glanced to the sky, estimating a few more hours of light. The days were longer as spring edged toward summer.

Flashing Kemper's picture and asking questions would only draw the wrong kind of attention to the woman he was meant to protect. Dallas locked his truck and pocketed the key fob. Better to explore on foot. He circled the block, chatted with the one man locking up the plumbing supply place. "I just bought a storage unit franchise," he lied to the plumber. "Looking for the right place to park it. My first location fell through."

"This'd be a good spot," the plumber said. "Things move fast though." He tipped his head to the construction across the street. "They say that'll be a brewery in a few months."

"You're kidding." Dallas looked up and down the street. "Weird spot for that."

"Zoning laws. Claims he'll get traffic from folks on their way to and from the park."

"Huh." Dallas followed the man's gaze up the street toward the brown sign with mileage information for the national forest. "Guess he might be on to something." He smiled. "Thanks for your time."

Had she dared to take a ride with someone headed out of town? Kemper wasn't outside this area, although she might be hiding inside one of the stores. If she'd headed for the park, Tyler wouldn't have lost her at this intersection. There were cameras on the construction site as well as the plumbing supply building. Either way, the motel was worth a look. He strolled up the street.

The clerk behind the desk wasn't inclined to share information about the check-ins for the day until Dallas added a hefty dose of charm to the twenties he offered.

No one matching Marnie's description had checked in, but the clerk did give Dallas a list of currently booked rooms. He walked the length of the building, starting with the first floor, pausing at the rooms that were supposedly occupied. Between the noise on the road and the hum and whirs of the individual heating and cooling units for each room, it wasn't easy to pick out the sounds of people.

Nearing the stairwell, he heard voices. Too young, too happy, and too many to be the woman he was here to protect. He let them pass overhead before he continued his stroll. None of the rooms downstairs that should be vacant showed signs of life.

Starting up to the second floor, he checked his list. There were two families booked in adjoining rooms at one end of the building. That must've been the kids he'd heard earlier, traveling in a pack to the vending machines that were located in a central alcove.

Access to a freight elevator and a supply office were behind the vending area for guests. He tested the office door. Locked. Not that it would be a stretch to pick it, but there were no signs of tampering. The freight elevator panel showed a security key-access. He pressed the button anyway, unsurprised when nothing happened.

Moving along toward the rooms closer to the motel office, his instincts kicked into a higher gear. Where else could she be but here? If she'd walked or hitch-hiked, or even hidden in one of the stores, Tyler would've found her on area cameras. Tyler and the gun man hunting her.

Dallas's mind raced through the litany of what-ifs that were in store once he found her. What if she had more information? What if she'd been turned? What if he was too late?

Those were just the top three.

He heard someone moving quickly on the walkway behind him and he braced for a fight. The man passed by when Dallas paused at the next door, pretending to fumble with his key at the door. Turning just enough to get a description without raising suspicion, he took note of the dark suit, lean build, and bald head.

He knocked on the door, as if calling to someone inside while he watched the bald man wrestle with another door, jiggling the knob and shoving at the door with his shoulder. The door gave, but the chain held. The man's tone of frustration was clear, though the specific words were not.

Logically, Dallas knew plenty of bald men wore dark suits on any given day. The man might be completely legit. His instincts insisted there was more to it. He stepped closer. "Got a problem?"

The bald man didn't spare him a glance, he pulled out a gun, the barrel lengthened by a silencer, and fired into the opening limited by the chain. Killers came in all shapes and sizes and although it helped to be smart, they weren't always.

Predictably, he hadn't hit whoever he was targeting in the room. The door closed on the gunman and he yelped, swearing a blue streak.

Dallas saw other doors opening, guests curious about the ruckus amplified by the block walls and concrete walkway. He wasn't an MP anymore and innocent bystanders weren't exactly his priority. Still, he shouted for people to stay inside as he launched himself at the gunman.

Their combined weight broke the chain lock and they landed in a heap inside the room.

The gun was kicked aside by a dark shoe, but that was the extent of the details Dallas could collect while he fought the bald man.

They rolled, giving Baldy the advantage. Steely fingers gripped his throat, crushing his windpipe while the man's bony knees dug into his ribs. Sips of air kept him conscious. With both fists, he struck Baldy at the elbows and sucked in a deep breath as he rolled to the side, gaining an advantage.

He saw the flash of blond hair, assumed it belonged to his assignment as he slammed the Baldy's gleaming head against the door frame. The blow stunned him and he oozed to the floor in a heap.

"Are you Marnie Kemper?" Dallas demanded as he searched the gunman for any identification or additional weapons.

"Yes," she replied, her voice steady.

"Good. Hamilton sent me." He found a knife in the man's belt and tossed it deeper into the room. Removing a small revolver from the man's ankle holster, he tucked that into his back pocket. "I'm—"

"Step away from him."

Dallas looked up. Marnie had Baldy's gun aimed at his chest, center mass, as if she'd been through law enforcement training. "I'm here to help," he said, keeping his voice low and soothing. Had she been turned? "I'm on your side."

"Prove it."

She had the prettiest eyes he'd ever seen. Even narrowed in suspicion, those eyes were a gorgeous, clear blue, framed by thick lashes and burnished gold eyebrows several shades darker than her hair. He could drown in her gaze, like sliding into a deep glacial lake, and call it bliss.

"Come on," she demanded, her scowl hard. "Give me ID or something."

If he reached back, his hand would be too close to the gun. He wouldn't give her that much reason to fire on him. "You might have noticed I'm not trying to kill you," he pointed out. "I even stopped that guy from doing so." He spread his hands out wide and turned slightly. "I'm going to hand you my identification." Slowly, though everything inside him screamed to get out of here fast, he reached for his wallet and held it out to her.

She snatched it from his fingers, the gun still trained on his heart.

At his feet, the man groaned and he kicked him in the ribs to keep him down.

"Be nice," she said. "Mr. Winston?"

Nice? Murderous Baldy hadn't earned an ounce of nice. "That's right. Call me Dallas. I'm a bodyguard with the Guardian Agency. The agency sent me to help you," he explained. "We really need to get moving." He did *not* want to get caught up in the red tape of the local law enforcement.

"I didn't call for a bodyguard. I've never heard of you."

"We work on referral only. I was told the U.S. Attorney made the request when no one could find you after the shooting at the courthouse." The barrel of the gun dipped as her arm grew tired. "Can I at least drag this guy inside, out of the doorway? We're drawing too much attention."

"Do what you want," she said. "I'm leaving."

She threw the gun at him, followed by his wallet, and darted through the doorway. He knocked the gun down, let the wallet fall, and caught her around the waist, hauling her up against him.

He stumbled, blaming it on the annoying nerve in his leg rather than the feel of her body in his arms. Stupid nerve. Pushing her behind him, he kicked the gunman to the walkway and pushed the door closed, though it didn't stay that way. That would give the cops a momentary distraction if he couldn't get her out of here.

He kept her tight against his side as he retrieved his wallet. "Miss Kemper, we need to leave. Together. For your safety."

"I can take care of myself," she said squirming.

Heat flashed through his veins with the grind of her hips against his pelvis and thigh. He wasn't a randy teenager, he was a professional, damn it. Something about her pushed all of his buttons and left him struggling for self-control. This had never been a problem before and he'd protected some beautiful women since joining the agency.

"Do you hear the sirens?" he asked at her ear.

"Yes." She sounded breathless, as if she'd just sprinted across a finish line.

"If you trusted the police, I assume you would've waited for help at the courthouse."

She nodded. "He told me to run."

"Who?"

"Jerry. My security escort. He's…is he dead?"

Dallas hated to make a bad day worse. "Yes." Her body went lax and he tightened his arm to keep her upright against him. "You've done well to last this long with this killer on your trail. Trust me now and I *will* get you out of here in one piece."

"I-I can't."

Dallas was losing his patience. "You are in serious trouble, Ms. Kemper. I can get you out of here. Once we're clear, I'll let you call anyone you like until you're satisfied that I'm your best chance to survive."

Her head came up and her spine stiffened as the sirens grew closer. "Fine."

She pushed away from him and grabbed the gunman's knife. "Problem?"

His let his gaze wander over her, not in a lecherous way, but taking precious seconds to really observe her. She held the knife like a pro and he decided she could probably hold her own, especially with the adrenaline that was coursing through her system. Though he had reach and weight advantages, he wouldn't underestimate her. "Not unless you plan on taking a slice out of me."

"I won't."

He didn't quite believe her. In her place, he'd demand the revolver. He was grateful she didn't. The best way to gain her trust was to extend some trust to her. "Let's go."

The first patrol car was skidding into the parking lot when he peeked out the door. The gunman was gone, leaving behind a few drops of blood on the concrete. Dallas didn't harbor any illusions that the killer had given up on Marnie.

"Plan B." He moved a chair in front of the door to keep it closed.

"You had a plan A?"

"Of course," he replied. By accident or design, she'd hidden in a room that connected to the room next door. It was the break they needed. He picked the lock instead of busting through the flimsy divide. The adjoining room, also unoccupied thankfully, was a corner space, with an extra window that overlooked the back of the motel. Moving quickly, he locked the main door with the chain and deadbolt.

"Are we staying?" she asked, clearly skeptical of his abilities.

"You live in Eagle Rock, right?"

"That's right," she replied.

"So you've probably heard of Hank Patterson," Dallas continued.

"I have." She folded her arms over her chest. "He's a former SEAL and he established the Brotherhood Protectors."

"That's right." Not his point, he just wanted to keep her talking and engaged. He went to the window near the door, jerking back when he spotted a policeman coming around the corner of the building.

"A friend of mine works with Patterson," Dallas said, hoping it would be an effective endorsement. "Do you do any rock climbing? Camping?" He didn't hear her answers, his mind on the potential pain of going out the window. It would hurt like hell, but he didn't see another way. Blood trail or not, the police would search the entire motel, starting with the rooms closest to where the fight had been.

He peered out the window again, swearing when he saw the gunman creeping up on the cop watching the rear of the motel. He couldn't let the officer get blindsided.

Pulling the revolver from his back pocket, he checked the chamber. Full load. Convenient. "I'll shoot out the window," he improvised. He'd rather not tell her the killer was still close. "That will draw their attention and we'll go out the front door."

She arched one golden eyebrow. "That easy?"

"Better to hope for the best," he said. What a hackneyed philosophy. One he rarely employed. He'd spent most of his life braced for the worst. From his family, the reservation, and the world in general. Just when he'd found his feet with a career and a partner, they'd been shot up, a beautiful partnership snuffed out by a quick burst of gunfire.

Dallas had tried to get back to active duty, even without a K9 partner, but his leg kept interfering with the physical demands. Now he wondered if the Army was right. Could he actually do his job and get Marnie out of here in one piece?

CHAPTER 3

MARNIE STUDIED the man who was supposedly her rescuer. Dallas Winston talked a good game and she couldn't argue with his results, but part of her worried it was a ruse. Someone had told a killer where she'd be and when. Someone had killed the man guarding her. Knowing the reputation of the criminal organization at the heart of this case, it wasn't a stretch to think Dallas might also be a trap.

Would he seriously shoot out one window so they could stroll away through the door? It couldn't be that easy. The police wouldn't send everyone around to the back of the motel.

Did she have a better choice? She could run toward the police and try to explain the mess and the weapons along with her illegal presence in the room, but after this morning, she didn't know who to trust. Maybe it was stress or fear or another tide of panic, but the bodyguard's diversion seemed solid. She'd break away from him at the first opportunity and find her own way back home.

The best choice became the only choice when he shot through the window, the sound and odor of gunpowder filling the room. The crack of the shattered glass was followed by an obscenely delicate tinkling as shards rained down on the pavement below.

A flurry of movement on the walkway outside followed. Boots rushed away from the door. Raised voices made demands and replies came back through crackling radios.

It couldn't have been more than a few seconds, though Marnie felt as if minutes were passing between her heartbeats. Every sound and sensation was separate, distinct. Fear was a strange counterpoint to logic and had been warping her sense of time since she fled the courthouse.

Dallas kept firing through the window. She jumped, stifling a scream as time slammed back to normal. "What are you doing?" Torn, she moved closer. If he was shooting cops, she would absolutely use the knife and hold him for arrest.

"Stay back." His free arm pinned her behind him and he took them both to the floor as police shouted for him to cease fire.

"That's our cue." In a crouch, he hustled her toward the front door.

She let him take the lead. Why not? Her life was

screwed beyond recognition. This morning a valuable witness, now a fugitive. *If* she got out of here alive, she'd have to become a totally new person. How she'd manage that was a problem for later.

Survival first.

To her shock, his ploy had worked. They made it out of the room and down the stairs near the front office without being spotted by authorities.

"Now the hard part," he muttered.

"Now?" she asked, incredulous. "We were trapped in there. *Now* we're free."

"It's a long way to my truck." His eyes were such a dark brown that the irises nearly blended with his pupils. His gaze was trained on the parking lot across the street.

"If we split up, we might have a chance," she suggested.

"No way."

His large hand gripped her arm just above her elbow and she shivered at the contact. Her denim jacket wasn't nearly enough protection from the heat of his palm. To her dismay, her body took a swift and full inventory of his. He had to be just over six foot tall and his thick black hair was trimmed close and pushed back from his face. His stern expression only emphasized the slash of dark eyebrows, straight nose and sharp chin. Strength oozed from every inch of him in an athletic capable way. She fought the urge to lean in to the shelter of his body and blamed this new insanity on adrenaline.

"Davis—"

"Dallas," he corrected.

"I can surrender and explain while you get out of here."

"No way," he repeated. "Your life is my responsibility."

She recoiled, shivering. Her security detail had said the same thing and now Jerry was dead. Dallas didn't notice her resistance. Shrugging out of his olive green windbreaker, he draped it over her shoulders. His scent enveloped her and the fabric, warm from his body, took the edge off the chill she hadn't been able to shake all day.

He tried to put his sunglasses over his eyes, but a cracked lens and bent frame were hopeless. Rather than toss them away, he hooked them onto his shirt collar. "To the corner. We'll cross at the light and then turn toward the plumbing supply building."

She was sure her spine would snap any second, she was strung so tightly waiting for the bullet. The protest she should've made died on her tongue when his fingertips landed protectively at the small of her back. He guided her with the lightest of touches, though she hadn't forgotten his directions or the feel of those words brushing against her ear and cheek.

Every step was surreal, an unexpected delight to still be alive. She turned as instructed, the pressure of his fingers unnecessary, but a welcome reminder that she wasn't out here alone. Assuming he was the real deal and she could trust him.

What would happen when they reached his truck? She prayed she hadn't just exchanged one deadly chapter of this nightmare for another.

He guided her around to the passenger side of a beautiful, well-kept silver pickup and opened the door.

"Are we on a date?" she said, feeling surly.

"I'd like anyone watching to think so," he replied with remarkable ease. Then his eyes cooled, his jaw set. He braced a hand on the frame and leaned closer. "Do not run," he said. "I'll only catch you and it will draw unwanted attention."

"As long as you get me out of here in one piece, we can renegotiate terms later."

He lingered there, his dark eyes unfathomable as he contemplated her reply. At last he shoved back, out of her space. She took her first steady breath in too long, reaching for her seatbelt as he closed the door firmly between them.

He watched her through the glass for a beat, then rounded the hood of the truck, his gaze locked on her. She wasn't without ingenuity or self-defense skills, but she was grateful for him and starting to believe that he'd been sent by someone who had her best interests in mind.

He climbed into the cab, his mouth twisting as he settled behind the wheel.

"Are you hurt?" she asked.

"No more than usual," he replied with a sigh. "Don't worry about me."

She wouldn't. And she'd ignore the bruises starting to show above the collar of his navy button-down shirt. Her body quaked as he pulled out onto the main road, driving out of town, toward the national forest recreational area.

"You're welcome to verify my credentials." He handed her his cell phone, showing her the screen was unlocked. "I don't have any secrets. Make yourself at home with my search history if it helps."

She turned the phone over and over in her hands. Feeling safe, breathing a bit easier, she had to face facts. If he hadn't intervened, she might have been killed by the gunman. "Why are you doing this?"

"It's my job, Ms. Kemper. I was hired to protect you and that is my sole focus."

She stared at his phone. Snooping wasn't her thing, yet she really should verify his claim. She wished she knew who to call. "You shot repeatedly at the policemen."

"I'm sure it looked that way." His long fingers curled around the steering wheel. "I shot at the man who attacked you to warn the policeman watching the rear that he had company."

"And to create a diversion."

"Two birds, one stone." He shrugged, as if he made those kinds of choices every day.

He was quiet for a long time and though it made sense to take him up on his offer to search his phone, she wasn't sure what good it would do. She'd long passed exhausted and didn't have any faith in her ability to sort fact from fiction. All she wanted was to curl up and sleep off the adrenaline rush. Trusting him blindly probably made her a fool, but evasion on her own hadn't been working so well either.

"How do you think the killer found me?"

"Probably the same way we did," he replied. "Check my call logs." He pointed at the phone. "You'll see the name Tyler. He's my agency research assistant and tech support. Go ahead and call him."

She knew she should, but what would calling a contact in his phone prove? Instead, she took a chance and dialed the number for her best friend, putting the call on speaker when Edie answered. Edie was her business partner with the café and quite possibly the better cook. She'd been keeping things running since the FBI placed Marnie into protective custody.

"Hello?"

Edie's familiar voice brought tears to Marnie's eyes. They hadn't spoken in months. "Hi, Edie." She swallowed. "Hi. It's—"

"Marnie!" Edie's voice dropped to a fierce whisper. "Oh, my God. Are you okay? The shooting in Helena is all over the news."

Over the phone, she caught the dark scowl on

Dallas's face. "I'm all right for the moment. Can you do me a favor?"

"Anything," Edie replied.

"Can you ask Hank Patterson if he knows, um, Dallas Winston? Please? Just call me back at this number." She ended the call before Edie could reply.

"You think someone tapped her phone or mine?" Dallas queried.

"I think anything is possible," she said. "Today proves the theory that sometimes paranoia is the wisest response."

The man who'd rescued her was almost as handsome in profile as he was face to face. His deeper skin had a healthy golden hue, as if the sun had graced him personally. To her eye his features and build pointed to a Native American lineage and she wondered if he was connected to her case. Maybe the leaders of Autumn Curley's tribe had sent him to ensure justice would prevail.

She opened her mouth to ask when the phone rang in her hand. Edie's phone number flashed across the screen. Dallas used the button on the steering wheel to answer the call before she could tap the icon.

"Marnie?"

"Right here, Edie. You're on speaker. Sorry about hanging up on you."

"Don't be," her friend replied. "I get it. Okay. Hank doesn't know him personally, but he told me that Joe Kuntz vouches for him."

Interesting. She caught the way Dallas gripped the wheel a little tighter. Joe, his dog Six, and Joe's wife Molly, were among her favorite regular customers. "What about Six?"

Edie chuckled. "I assume he would vote with Joe but I can always call and verify."

"He wouldn't," Dallas murmured. "Six didn't like me when we met."

What did he mean by that?

"Hank also told me that someone named Tyler who works with Mr. Winston called and asked him to keep an eye out for you here. Are you coming back?"

"I will," Marnie promised. She was determined to take back her life just as soon as she delivered her testimony and this case was closed. "I won't be in protective custody forever. Thanks, Edie," she said, ending the call without further explanation.

There. Now anyone who was listening would be scrambling to figure out if she was on the road to Eagle Rock or back in a safe house. With a little luck, that could buy her time to get to safety.

"Feel better?" he asked.

"I wish I could say yes without reservation." Her bones ached, her muscles were screaming from a day filled with fear. "I am less worried you're going to kill me."

Dallas's mouth kicked into a wry grin. "They wouldn't keep me on the payroll if I was in the habit of doing the work for the bad guys."

As an endorsement it wasn't much comfort. "How do you know Joe?" And more importantly, why wouldn't Six like him?

Again, his hand tightened on the steering wheel and he fidgeted in his seat. For the longest time, she thought he wouldn't answer. "When I was in the Army I was an MP and worked with a K9 partner. We met with our partners during a refresher course."

"And Six didn't like you?" She should stifle her curiosity, but she counted Joe and Six as friends.

"He wasn't with Six then," Dallas said.

It wasn't much of an explanation. "And you're not in the Army anymore."

He reached up and tapped a panel in the ceiling and withdrew a pair of sunglasses, settling them over his eyes. Grief was etched into the hard line of his jaw. "Correct."

"Oh." She felt like a complete jerk as a dozen new questions bubbled up. She wouldn't ask, though she wanted to hear the whole story. "I'm sorry for your loss." She didn't need all the details to see something bad had separated him from his partner and ended his military career.

He swiveled his head to look at her, the sunglasses shielding his eyes before he faced the road again. "Where were they keeping you?" he asked. "Before they brought you back for the trial."

She propped her elbow against the door and rested her cheek on her hand. "Idaho Falls. They were pushing the case along, so for the last few months, I've been stuck in a safe house with the team."

"No one told you that you'd have to give up all ties to Eagle Rock and start over somewhere else?"

She sat up straight and stared at him. "Not once. My plan was always to testify and go back home. It wasn't a secret. Jerry and the others on the team told me it would work out."

"Huh."

"Meaning?"

"Take it easy, Ms. Kemper."

"Marnie," she snapped.

"Marnie," he repeated.

He said her name as if he'd covered it in honey and her skin tingled. She fought to focus on what else he was saying.

"I'm just surprised. From what I know about the case, the criminals behind the trafficking ring could keep a bounty on your head for years."

"Gee, thanks for that comforting thought."

"Wishing you'd settled for 'huh'?"

"More than a little."

She studied him, trying to hide how absorbed she was with the way his hands moved over the steering wheel, how he checked the mirrors and shifted in his seat. He had long limbs, a graceful presence, and the edge of a tattoo near his wrist. Did his shirt cover a fully-inked arm?

"Come to any conclusions?" he asked.

"Pardon me?"

"You've been staring for the past three miles. I wondered if you'd come to any conclusions about me or whatever is on your mind."

Heat flooded her face and she was grateful only the glow of the gauges on the dashboard lit the cab. "No, no," she sputtered. "No conclusions. You aren't any of my business."

Her curiosity about him was simply a byproduct of her ordeal. She *wasn't* curious about *him*. She only wanted to know why Hamilton believed he was the right man to rescue her and keep her safe until the trial.

"I've been a bodyguard for a couple of years now," Dallas volunteered. "Haven't lost anyone yet and I won't botch my perfect record with you. Count on that."

"Okay," she said.

"My K9 partner was killed when a drug bust went sideways," he said. "After the, ah, incident, it was clear I needed a career change. This works."

"You don't owe me an explanation." She didn't need to know him, didn't want to get too close. Yes, she'd befriended the men and women on her security team, mainly because they were the only other people to talk with. Now Jerry was dead. It didn't take a detective to figure out someone else on the team, someone she'd trusted, had shared her location so she could be killed before testifying.

"What do you know about my situation?" she asked.

"Only the basics about you in particular," he said, leaning forward in his seat and then settling back. "I've followed the Curley case closely. You saved a young woman from hell on earth."

"That's a big leap," Marnie said. Such praise always left her uncomfortable. The whole situation had landed in her lap. She hadn't done anything remarkable or noble, she'd only been willing to do the right thing. "Autumn had the guts to create an escape opportunity. I let her use the phone, let her hide in my office when her captors came looking for her."

"As I said."

She shook her head, suddenly weary. It was as if her energy and courage had faded away with the setting sun. "Is protecting me personal for you?"

"You're asking if I volunteered for this assignment because the victims in the case are primarily Native American women and girls."

"Yes," she replied. "No. It's not a judgment," she added, in case he was inclined to slap a racist label on her. Not anywhere close to accurate, but she was too tired, her thoughts too jumbled, to state her feelings the right way. Yes, his heritage made his features different from hers. She was a cookie-cutter white girl with blonde hair and blue eyes courtesy of her Scandinavian roots. Neither of them had a say in their ancestry. Appearance wasn't her issue, hope was. Hope that because of his cultural connection to the victim he might have extra motivation to keep her alive.

"And people say the Wild West is dead," he said.

"I don't care what you look like," she snapped. "I'm hoping your potential connection to the victims means you won't sell me out."

His lengthy silence gave her plenty of time to wallow in her ungraciousness as he drove deeper into the protected land of the national forest. "Where are we going?" she asked as he turned off the paved road.

"I didn't hear your answer earlier. Based on your file, I assumed you enjoyed camping."

That was more than a little disconcerting, although he'd admitted to knowing her basics. "You're right. I do."

"Good." He pressed the heel of his hand to his hip and shifted in the seat again.

"Are you okay?"

"Fine," he replied. "It's a grumpy nerve. Tries to get the better of me." He pointed when his headlights hit the sign. "There's a campground up here. We'll sleep in the truck tonight and make a better plan tomorrow."

She was supposed to sleep here, in the truck, with him? "What about security or..." Deadbolts. Alarms. Steel doors. She couldn't finish the sentence. All the reasonable responses were like a logjam between her brain and mouth.

"Marnie?"

She chewed on her lip.

"Look at me, Marnie." The truck rocked as he pulled into an open camp site and cut the engine. "I *am* your security." The campground bathhouse was directly in front of them. "No one followed us. No one knows we're here. You're safe with me."

If only it was as easy as believing him. "Did you kill the man who found me at the hotel?"

"No." He swiveled in his seat, resting one arm on the steering wheel. "He was too close to the cop when I fired. I couldn't chance it."

She couldn't let the worry go. "Then he might have seen us leave. He might know this vehicle."

His chest swelled as he inhaled deeply. He reached out and stilled her restless hands. "You'll be safe with me," he said again. "I keep a spare toiletry kit for clients, if you want to freshen up while I deal with the tent."

Through the windshield, she stared at the bathhouse. Could she go in there alone? Night had claimed the sky and the light at the doors wasn't bright enough to chase away the shadows surrounding them. She sighed. At this point, the sun might not be bright enough to counter her fears. For the first time in her life, she didn't want to camp, didn't find any peace or comfort in the solitude of nature.

"This is where I was headed," she heard herself say. "Not this particular campground, but the park."

"Great minds think alike." He smiled as he opened his door and rooted around behind the seat. He pulled out a small tote and handed it to her. "Use whatever you need. We can restock and do some shopping tomorrow."

"Thanks."

A bit more rustling and a cooler appeared. "Nothing fancy. Or cold," he added sheepishly. "But it's sustenance."

Her appetite was non-existent. Apparently her stomach had given up on her. She wasn't sure she could keep anything down at this point. "Thanks," she said again.

He walked away and her heart banged around in her chest, a frightened bird unable to fly away. With a dull clang, the tailgate dropped open and Dallas hopped up into the truck bed.

She should help him with the tent. She should do something more than offer weak thanks for his handling everything. Instead, she left the truck for the bathhouse, relieved when her movements caused another light to pop on and illuminate more of the area.

Though she'd washed the blood from her hands earlier, she scrubbed them again and splashed cool water over her face. Drying off with the towel provided, she fought back a wave of useless tears when her gaze landed on her blood-spattered shirt.

It was selfish to be upset. People wanted her dead, unable to testify. That wasn't a new revelation. Her ordeal hardly compared to the evil Autumn had seen and survived. Sure, Marnie's life was upside-down, but it was a temporary turmoil. Thanks to Edie, business was thriving.

Marnie had dealt with the isolation of protective custody, ever-confident she'd get back to Eagle Rock and her life and friends. Being aware, being hopeful hadn't changed any of the facts or the risks. Today, a man she considered a friend had sacrificed himself for her, for the case. His life snuffed out between one heartbeat and the next while they debated lunch stops. She was standing here, alive, thanks to Jerry. And Dallas.

She should be full of gratitude. Instead her reflection was a picture of fear and uncertainty. How had the woman she'd been, the smiling outgoing person, disappeared so quickly? Maybe she'd never been that woman at all. Maybe *that* reflection had been the lie and the real Marnie Kemper was insecure, self-centered, and whiny. Suspicious of everything and a verifiable risk to everyone near her.

Worry carved ragged lines across her forehead and around her mouth. It dawned on her as she challenged that woman in the mirror. No matter who she'd been before today, she was forever altered by today's tragic, terrifying events. She didn't want her customers in Eagle Rock to see this hard, weathered version of her face.

The first tear trembled on her lashes and when it spilled over, the dam broke. Her entire body shook with the force of her wrecked emotions and she sank to the floor between the sinks, covering her face with her hands, trying to smother the wretched sounds.

Dallas had boldly charged into the role of new bodyguard. He'd declared it with conviction and she repeated it over and over, trying to soothe herself. He'd promised to keep her safe, keep her alive, so she could testify. She sobbed harder, wrapping her arms around her knees.

She pressed her face into the damp towel and an image of Dallas bleeding out assaulted her. Marnie couldn't pretend that wasn't a possible outcome. A likely outcome.

Putting more people in the crosshairs wasn't fair. He seemed like a generally nice person. Polite. Definitely competent. And strikingly beautiful. She should leave, put some distance between them. The criminals determined to silence her clearly didn't care about collateral damage. She couldn't bear the idea of another person taking a bullet meant for her.

She needed to rescue herself. Dallas had given her a good head start and it was up to her now. She would run and he could go help someone else. Out in the wilderness she could survive long enough for the noise to die down. It wouldn't be easy, but better to rough it alone than put friends and family and gorgeous bodyguards in danger.

Her mind made up, she hauled herself upright and went to the door to check on Dallas. He was near the cab of the truck and a tent had been raised in the truck bed. A soft lantern glowed on a hook near the tailgate. Such a normal scene made her want to cry again. If she was going, this was her opening.

The campground bathhouse had doorways on both ends of the long building. She hurried to the far door, clutching the tote he'd given her. Leaving in the night with minimal gear wasn't ideal, but she couldn't shake the certainty that staying meant Dallas's blood would soon be on her hands too. She'd have to be quick. He would definitely notice when the motion-activated light on this end of the building came on. On a deep breath, she opened the door and ran. Right into the hard wall of muscle that was Dallas.

CHAPTER 4

DALLAS CAUGHT Marnie for the second time and it was no less electrifying than the first. He didn't stumble, a definite plus, and her soft curves were a snug, perfect fit against him. He should step back to arm's length. Instead, he held her close in his arms. She couldn't escape, but then neither could he.

"Tent's ready." His jaw, his voice, hell all of him was tight with wanting her. The temptation to demand an explanation coursed through his system. Almost as powerful as the temptation to kiss her tantalizing mouth.

Being attracted to a client wasn't unheard of, but it wasn't ideal and it wasn't the least bit professional. He loosened his grip and felt her muscles shift. Fight or flight? He kept his hands on her waist, waiting for her next move.

Would she try and bolt again? Where did she think

she could go? His job was to keep her safe from any threat. That included the threat of fear that prompted irrational action. Ignoring the universal icon of a woman painted on the door, he marched her back into the bathhouse and through the door closest to his truck.

The silence snapped and sizzled between them.

He kept his arm around her waist, his fingers locked into that sweet slope above her hip. Her leg brushed his as they walked, her arm bumping into his ribs. Semi-hard and irritated with himself, he was grateful for the long shadows that hid his reaction to her. He didn't give her any extra room until they reached his truck.

"I'd planned to sleep in the cab," he said, unzipping the tent flap. "Give you some privacy."

She stared up at him, her teeth working over her full lower lip. He dragged his gaze back to her eyes, dragged his thoughts away from the pros and cons of kissing her. Her eyes were puffy, a sure sign she'd been crying. Something in his chest twisted uncomfortably. Tears were *not* his specialty, though emotions often ran high with clients in danger.

"Looks like I'd better sleep back here," he said.

"On the ground? No. You don't have to do that." Her voice was flat, the words hardly convincing. "I promise to stay put."

Damn it. He wanted to believe her. Not just because the nerve in his leg would complain all day tomorrow if he slept on the bare ground tonight. He raised his chin, urging her up into the tent. She turned to obey and he ruthlessly stifled the groan when her butt was at eye-level as she crawled into the shelter. So close. He shoved his hands into his pockets. So close and absolutely off limits.

"Were you running from me?" he asked when she plopped down in the center of the air mattress.

"No. Yes. Not exactly."

He waited for clarification and was disappointed. Her lack of acknowledgement about the setup irked him. He'd worked double-time to get the tent up, the bed inflated, and the other gear arranged for her comfort. Why he expected praise or thanks irritated him further. She was a client, scared and overwhelmed. Basic manners often went out the window under such circumstances. Even he had to be more direct or tactile in certain instances. He had no right to expect Marnie to be different.

"Get some sleep." He'd put a blanket in the cab, where it would have to stay for the night. No way was he giving her an opening to run again. "I'll be right here keeping watch. Rest well."

He zipped the tent flap closed, unable to blot out the sweet fantasy of stretching out beside her, getting a taste of her lush mouth. Resigned to a rough, cold night, he felt her watching him as he turned out the lantern. Her attention heated him up in inappropriate places as he turned and stretched out under the tailgate. His back and hip would be miserable by morning.

Maybe it would be helpful if she did sneak away. Tracking her on foot would give his body a good healthy challenge.

"You're angry with me." Her voice whispered through the tent, across his senses, no relief at all for his unrelenting attraction. "Not angry," he countered. "Concerned is more accurate."

"Because you're obligated to get me back to the courthouse in one piece?"

He heard her shifting on the mattress and pictured her curled up on her side, blonde hair pushed back from her face, a hand tucked under her chin. Too bad he'd never know if he was right or wrong. "I'm not a bounty hunter, you didn't skip bail." She knew that. "My job is to keep you safe. Alive. That's the extent of my agenda."

Well, look at that. He could still spin a lie with ease. His only *professional* agenda was keeping her alive. Certain parts of his anatomy were clamoring about much different ways to fill the days until it was time for her to testify. His palms tingled at the thought of touching her, exploring the silky texture of her skin or the way her supple curves would melt under his touch. Despite the darkness, it was a wonder she couldn't see his desire rippling in the air like heat rising from the pavement on a scorching day.

"Dallas, what if I don't want to be protected?"

Her voice was so faint he thought he'd imagined it.

"Dallas? Did you hear me?"

His imagination would've filled in a more enticing conversation. Why wouldn't she want protection? "I thought you were smarter than that."

The mattress squeaked against the tent floor as she moved again. "What do you mean?" Her voice was closer now, just overhead.

"You're educated," he said, sitting up. "You've built up a successful business. Of course you want to be protected."

"Do I?" Another soft shift. "The café is doing just fine without me."

"Don't you want it back?" He couldn't figure out what she needed to hear.

"Yes."

He liked the strength and conviction she packed into that single word. "Then let me help you. Let me keep you safe so you *can* go back."

She sniffled. "A man died today. Right beside me. *Because* of me."

Ah, guilt was the crux of the issue. He'd become a pro at unraveling this type of twisted thought process. He'd take guilt over tears any day, any case. "That doesn't mean your situation will be the death of *me*."

"How can you know for sure?"

Sheer arrogance was part of it, along with confidence in his abilities and a successful track record. "Experience," he said. "We got out of the motel, right?"

"Yes. Thank you."

He couldn't force her to see that the hardest part,

escape, was over. Evasion with a healthy head start was inconvenient but easier as long as they stayed smart. "So why did you try to run?"

A snuffling snort was the first reply. Please not more tears. He'd never handled crying women with much skill and definitely not when he wanted to be kissing said woman.

"You're too pretty to die," she said.

The statement was ludicrous. Or he was overtired. Either way, he started laughing, a deep belly laugh he couldn't contain.

"That isn't a joke," she said, indignant. She unzipped the tent flap and scooted forward to glare at him.

He kept right on laughing through her protests. "The same could be said for you," he managed when he caught his breath. She was more than pretty. She had an innately good nature. The world needed more people like Marnie Kemper. "Why be careless with your survival?"

"Now who's telling jokes?" she muttered. "Can we please part ways tomorrow? I can take care of myself until the trial."

Not a chance. He'd been hired to protect her and he'd work this case according to Guardian Agency protocol. "Go to sleep, Marnie. We'll talk it over in the morning," he said, still amused.

"Fine."

He heard the zipper on the tent flap, followed by

shifting and scooting of the mattress. Several more minutes passed before she was still, her breathing even.

Dallas wouldn't sleep much, if at all, unwilling to risk her slipping away while he was unconscious. He was used to cat-napping on a job. Still, he sent a text to Tyler, asking him to dig deeper into what made up Marnie Kemper's past. Anything that helped him understand her would help him protect her.

The pure shock of a bullet ripping through the person standing next to you would rattle anyone. No question about it. Worse if that person was a friend. But she seemed particularly worried that she'd turned into some sort of death magnet.

At the motes, he'd made the logical leap that someone close to the case had leaked her location to the bastards on trial. That didn't mean the protection order from the Guardian Agency had been compromised. They were camped, unregistered, in a national forest recreation area. The odds of being found here in the next few hours were ridiculously low.

Unless she was hiding something or she'd been bought off by the organization running the trafficking operation.

Hiding something, he could believe. Everyone had secrets. Cooperating with the bad guys didn't fit. He'd only met her a few hours ago, but the woman clearly had integrity. Without that, she wouldn't have done so much to assist Autumn Curley's escape. It took serious conviction and courage to testify against the men who'd come looking for their 'property'.

Plenty of witnesses backed out in cases like this one, whether or not the criminals threatened them directly.

He'd kept tabs on the case as it progressed. He wasn't privy to the depositions, only the official statements that Marnie stood by her account of the events and never wavered in her identifications. According to the information Tyler was gathering, the prosecution team had been immensely pleased by the practice session this morning.

Why was Marnie convinced they'd be compromised and something bad would happen to him? He'd like to blame her insistence on shock or fear, but aside from the obvious crying jag in the bathroom, she'd been cool and levelheaded.

Maybe she had feelings for the guy who'd taken a bullet today. Dallas sent Tyler another text to look into that as well. Then he tried his best to shut it all out and get a nap.

LIGHT FILTERED THROUGH THE TENT, gently waking Marnie. For a moment, the serene quiet of the new day fooled her into thinking life was normal. The air was clean and crisp with the scent of pine. Then she stretched and, with the squeak of the air mattress, yesterday's horrors came flooding back.

Shattered hope. The incomprehensible loss. Blood pooling on the steps, turning the mortar a dreadful, deep red.

If she got through this, she'd never pick up a gun again. As much as she enjoyed target practice and even hunting, she'd find a different hobby.

She paused, listening for any sign of Dallas, regretting that her rash escape attempt made him feel obligated to spend the night outside. She was ashamed for giving him another thing to worry about overnight. Keeping watch for a killer should've been more than enough.

Until the authorities found the man who'd killed Jerry and whoever had hired him, she was a threat to anyone around her. Even an experienced bodyguard. If Dallas wouldn't agree to let her protect herself until the trial, she'd just have to find some way to be more of an asset than a burden.

Sitting up, she yawned, stretched, and listened again. No sound of any movement near the truck. Panic zinged through her. What if the bald man had followed them? She froze in place, caught between leaping into action and wishing she could disappear. Before she could pull herself out of the morass of indecision, the zipper pull at the tent flap moved.

She hadn't heard anyone approach. Reaching for the knife she'd tucked between the mattress and the tent wall, she discovered it was gone. *Crap*. Defenseless in a truck tent was *not* how she planned to leave this world. No, she'd pictured a nice husband, a couple of sweet-faced kids, and decades of sunsets and hand-holding before she made her exit.

She wrapped her hand around her shoe, ready to use it as a club to save herself.

"Marnie?" Dallas's quiet voice cut through her anxiety a moment before his face appeared in the parted tent flap. "You're awake."

"You took the knife," she accused.

Immediately contrite, he offered it to her. "Only to make you think for a minute before you tried to run again."

"You left me defenseless."

"I didn't." He arched an eyebrow toward the shoe in her hands. "Pretty sure that would've worked in your favor, along with the element of surprise."

She slowly lowered the shoe, put it back on her foot. "You were close?"

"Always."

He leaned over and bounced the tailgate. Something jangled loudly and he reached down, lifting a thick chain. Somehow in the night, he'd taken her knife *and* manufactured an alarm of sorts with the tow chain. The sound and vibration would've woken her, startled an intruder and given them a chance to escape. How had he rigged it without waking her?

"Still want to part ways today?"

What a jerk to ask that now, when she was on edge and feeling cornered. "Yes." She didn't, but she'd never forgive herself if the killer hurt him. Or worse. "I know you think it's a crazy idea, but we really should," she said. "They're after me, not you."

His lips flattened into a line. Disappointment or disagreement? He extended a hand, beckoned her closer and helped her out of the tent.

"Take your time with a shower and whatever," he said. He handed her the tote again. "Then we'll talk it out."

She grabbed the tote and stalked off. Her mind was set on doing this her way. She was at the bathhouse door before she realized he wasn't beside her. "You trust me all of a sudden?"

"No," he admitted. The slow smile was devastating on that chiseled face.

She looked around, expecting to see reinforcements. He'd done something in the name of keeping her safe and present. She might not know him well, but he'd exhibited staying power and serious commitment. "What did you do?"

He only shook his head and resumed the process of packing up the tent. Whatever he had in mind for the day, it didn't involve staying here. What a relief.

The shower helped more than she wanted to admit. Clean clothes and real hiking gear would be even better, but without any resources she was stuck.

Unless she trusted Dallas.

Would he compromise at all? If he helped her get supplies to stay off the grid for the week until the trial, she'd let him escort her to the courthouse. Maybe. If he wore a bulletproof vest.

While brushing her teeth, she caught the flicker of a tiny red light mounted above the mirror. It looked a bit like a nanny cam thing. That hadn't been there last night. She glared at it as she finished her morning routine and then stormed back out to the campsite. Sure enough, Dallas was hurrying to tuck his cell phone into a pocket.

"You put a spy camera in the bathhouse."

"Sure did. I thought you might give me a hand and bring it out with you."

"Dallas!" She couldn't fault his sneakiness, and she couldn't claim that she felt violated, because she didn't. Not really. It hadn't been aimed in a direction that would've exposed her in a perverted way, only an attempt to escape.

She felt trapped and frustrated, but neither reaction had anything to do with him. Well, a little bit of the frustration was her increasing attraction. She couldn't go there. He was too hot for her and too sexy for her fantasies if she wanted to stay sane. As much as she wanted to grab him and kiss him until his sunglasses fogged over, she didn't want to *feel* anything for him. Feelings would only make things worse if he did get hurt taking care of her.

"We should get moving," he said. "I only have water and granola bars for breakfast, but we can get coffee or something else at the campground store." He nodded to the cab of the truck. "Stow the tote behind your seat."

She didn't budge. "You keep saying we'll talk."

"That's right." He hopped up into the truck bed. "We can talk while we drive."

Which kept him on duty and in the line of fire. Rather than arguing, she moved closer and watched him pack the camping gear into various storage compartments. "You've really customized this."

"Impressed?"

"Yes, actually."

"Good." He grinned down at her and her heart dropped to her toes. "Breakfast awaits." He gestured toward the cab. "I'll go grab the nanny cam and we're out of here."

Before she could reply, he was striding into the women's side of the bathhouse again. She opened the bottle of water and was fighting with the wrapper for the granola bar when it occurred to her she should've seized the opportunity to run.

Yes, he was too pretty to die for her. Clearly, he was also too tempting for her to keep a logical thought in her head.

Focused on his long stride, the hint of a smile on his lips, and the gorgeous morning reflected in his sunglasses, the splintering door behind him was a strange visual that didn't fit. Wood flew apart like something out of an action movie. The hard *crack* that followed a split-second later obliterated the sensual fog muddling her thoughts.

A bullet fired from a distance. Dallas dropped into a crouch, but he didn't stay down. There was no blood soaking his shirt when he reached her, shoved her into the truck, down between the seat and the dashboard. Within a few seconds the engine roared in her ears and they were moving, bouncing along the rough camp-ground road.

"You're not hit," she said, taking an inventory. His eyes were on the road, but he was the only thing she could see. The trees and sky in the windows behind his head were a blur.

"Stay low."

The tow chain, still loose in the truck bed, clanged and scraped from side to side as Dallas drove away from the shooter. Marnie made herself as small as possible, wishing she understood what was going on and why. The tires skidded on the gravel paths, finding purchase at last when he turned onto a paved road. The hum of rubber against the road blended into the rumble of the engine and she embraced the comfort of the reliable white noise.

By some miracle, the bullet had missed him. Maybe it had been meant for her and missed both of them. She clamped her lips together, holding back the scream that threatened to escape her fraying control. Screaming over Jerry hadn't changed anything yesterday and it sure wouldn't improve matters today.

"How did they find us?" Dallas's voice was as sharp as broken glass.

She didn't know. Didn't know why he expected her to have an answer.

"My guess is the traffic cameras," a new voice said. Not Dallas's voice, a stranger. She hadn't heard him make the call.

"Tyler," Dallas growled, "I need shelter and supplies. Off the grid."

Were there places more off the grid than the campground? It had seemed sufficiently removed and remote to her.

"Give me five minutes."

"I hope we have that long," Dallas muttered.

He didn't let up off the gas, the engine revving high at her ear. The vibration of the tires rolled up from the floorboard, through her entire body. She had no idea which tremors originated from the fear locked inside her and which were from outside forces. When he took the curves at speed, her body was pressed against the hard surfaces of the truck, first the seat frame, then the door, then the frame again. She'd come out of this with aches and bruises and she didn't care. As long as she came out alive.

He must have hit a straight patch because his big hand reached toward her. "Come on up here."

She grabbed him like the lifeline he was and let him help her into the passenger seat. Her hands fumbled, but she got the seatbelt to click. "It's safe now?"

He shook his head, checked his mirrors. "We seem to be out of firing range."

"Is that supposed to be comforting? Are there classes for that in your line of work?"

"Not exactly." He spared her a glance, one black eyebrow raised.

"There should be." Sniping at her rescuer wasn't kind and he'd been generous and capable. To a fault. "Sorry." Embarrassment warred with anger and guilt. "I'm really sorry."

"No need for apologies." His head moved as he checked the mirrors again. "A crisis requires direct and immediate action. I don't always make a smooth transition back to situation normal."

He had last night, once they were clear. "It's not you, it's me. Apparently fear makes me waspish. And you're obviously not sure the crisis is over."

"The immediate crisis *is* over," he confirmed. "But stopping for any touchy-feely stuff only gives them time to catch up."

"So what do we do?"

He actually growled. "We wait for options." His gaze cycled through the mirror rotation, pausing at the dash screen that would light up with an incoming call. They sailed around another curve and the engine labored at the sudden incline.

"I know this area," she said. "There's a turn-off not far from here."

"That leads where?"

"Parking for a trail head. A trail winds up toward a river overlook and a spur leads the opposite way to a shallow part of the river." It was a great place to go tubing or wading.

"Good signal strength for a cell phone?"

"I've never had cause to measure it," she said, matching his all-business tone.

She pointed to the intersection, but he drove right on by.

"Not stopping."

"Why not?"

"Anything that's too familiar to you is a risky solution. Whoever is after you seems well-informed."

"The campsite was your idea." She'd visited several times through the years, though, with friends and family.

"I'm aware," he muttered. "My idea and my mistake. Can't afford another one."

His lips pressed together, a muscle in his jaw jumping. Trouble or not, the man's profile was as striking as his face. It was hardly the time to notice. Or maybe it was the perfect time. Someone wanted her dead and she wasn't ready to go out on their terms. Admiring a handsome man was a lovely distraction.

She cleared her throat. "What did you see at the campsite?"

"Sniper fire aimed at you," he said.

"Interesting."

He turned, his lips parted in shock, before he gathered himself. "Explain."

She wished he'd take off the sunglasses. "I saw a bullet barely miss *your* shoulder, splintering the door behind you."

She lingered over the view of his profile while he pondered that. Having been raised in Montana, she'd met all manner of men. Rugged cowboys, slick investors, military veterans, the occasional celebrity, and Native Americans who either cherished traditions or eschewed their heritage had come in and out of her café.

Dallas didn't seem to fit neatly into any of one those categories. His heritage was clear in his chiseled features, dark eyes and that golden sun-warmed skin. His training shined in the calm way he handled himself in a crisis.

"Can't we just go to Eagle Rock?"

His body tensed so completely, so quickly, she swiveled in her seat, certain they'd been found, but they were the only car on the road.

"Not the smart move," he said.

She waved away the suggestion. "Chalk it up to fear-induced babbling." Still, why was the idea so out of line? "You'd have more backup there with Hank's men."

"I can handle this assignment," he said.

Great. Not only had she put him in danger, she'd managed to offend him. That probably put her at the top of his least-favorite client list. She started to apologize again when the sound of a ringing phone came through the truck speakers.

Dallas pressed the button on the steering wheel. "What did you find?"

"Pretty sure you were found because of the closed circuit system in the campground."

"I should have anticipated that," Dallas said.

"Businesses add them every day as the tech improves," his assistant said. "Plus, systems like the campground uses might as well be open source."

"How informative, Tyler," Dallas deadpanned. "What's my next best move?"

"First, you need to check your car for a GPS tag immediately. Second, when the car's clear, head straight for the White Oak ranch in Eagle Rock. Hank Patterson can help you with your next move."

Marnie's boost of happy energy at the thought of being home popped as the statement sunk in. They weren't talking about letting her go home, only making another move. "Has something happened?"

"Not specifically. We're monitoring the situation," Tyler said.

She didn't know the man on the other end of the call, but she heard the hesitation in his tone.

"What about getting her back for the trial?" Dallas asked. "Is that part of the 'next move' deal?"

"The trial dates are fluid right now," Tyler said.

"Spit it out," Dallas snapped. "We need all of the intel."

An exasperate sigh came through the speakers. "Two other witnesses are missing. Hamilton might have to ask for a continuance. Possibly drop the case."

"They have the depositions," Marnie blurted.

"Yes," Tyler said.

A flurry of emotion caught her heart in a painful vise. "Who is missing?"

"*Um.*" Tyler hesitated again. "Curley, the victim you protected, and another woman who witnessed the same two men in the act of a kidnapping."

Marnie wrapped her arms around her stomach. The young woman who'd walked into her café and hidden in her office when those men had come searching *was* the entire case. All these months later, the fear and desperation in Autumn's eyes that day still haunted Marnie's sleep. She couldn't imagine the horrors that young woman had survived. Marnie understood enough about the law to know that without Autumn, the men charged wouldn't get the full penalty they deserved for their crimes.

The case couldn't be falling apart. She'd put her trust in the system, expected justice to work. "No," she whispered, over and over.

If this case was dropped, a vile criminal group that traded women like a disposable commodity would be free to keep operating. She'd faced off against the men searching for Autumn, their threats still rang in her ears. Men like that didn't stop until they tied off every loose end.

Without successful prosecution, Autumn's courage, Marnie's support, and every brave witness would be worthless. Nothing she'd done had mattered. She couldn't bear it. Could. Not. Bear it.

She didn't realize Dallas ended the call or stopped the truck, didn't realize she was sobbing, until he was holding her, his T-shirt soaking up her uncontrollable tears.

Somehow he'd opened her door and unbuckled her seatbelt. She rested in his embrace, her head on his shoulder while he murmured soothing nonsense at her ear, one hand stroking her hair. The man didn't need any classes in offering comfort. He was clearly an expert, crisis or not.

Eventually, the tears subsided and she forced herself to pull back, wondering if she'd ever recover her dignity. Afraid of what she'd see in his eyes, she blotted her face with the collar of her shirt. "Sorry."

"Don't be."

How could he be so understanding? "An extended meltdown isn't helping the escape plan."

She heard a sound that might have been a chuckle. "No one's shooting at us yet," he said. "What do you want out of this, Marnie?"

"Justice," she replied instantly. "Justice for Autumn." She had to stop and get a grip on her emotions before another wave of tears swamped her. "For the other girls and women those men kidnapped and exploited. They all deserve justice."

"You're still willing to testify?"

She looked up at him then. He'd pushed his sunglasses up into his hair and she saw the gleam of determination in his dark gaze. It matched everything churning inside her. He bolstered her courage and confidence with that one look. It was enough to make her believe she could survive today, overcome the shock and fear to make sure the bastards were locked up for life.

"Hell, yes."

His chest rose on a deep inhale and she had the very inappropriate wish to see him do that without a shirt. What was wrong with her?

"All right. I can't guarantee justice. That's above my paygrade. I can't guarantee the next few days will be any kind of picnic, but I *will* keep you alive so you can testify. However long it takes."

"That works for me," she said. "Unfortunately, I can't guarantee that was the last meltdown."

He smiled, his dark eyes warming as his lips curved. The sexy expression left her weak-kneed and fluttery. She was glad she was sitting down or she might have oozed into a puddle of longing at his feet. Apparently dignity of any kind was out of the question around Mr. Guardian Agency.

"What happens to me if the case is dropped?"

His smile faded and his jaw firmed. His gaze drifted over the landscape behind her. "Logically, you wouldn't be a threat, especially to mid-level thugs on trial."

Logically. A chill slid down her spine, slowly bumping over each vertebra. The men who'd threatened her over Autumn hadn't struck her as the logical type. They'd want revenge for interfering with their cash flow. Would she spend the rest of her life looking over her shoulder?

"Hamilton said they hope one of the men will agree to testify against the people calling the shots and bankrolling the operation."

"It's a useful tactic," Dallas said.

"Go on."

He arched one eyebrow.

"I can see you have more opinions." She rubbed her arms. "You think whatever happens with the case, I'm a loose end they won't leave hanging."

He frowned and dropped his sunglasses back over his eyes.

"Killing you sends a bigger message," he said. "Makes it clear they won't tolerate Good Samaritans interfering with their plans. Too bad for them, you have me." He nudged her back into the truck. "Buckle up," he added before closing the door.

Her thoughts turned his words inside out while he searched the car for a GPS tracking device. She'd been a fool to think she could escape on her own. Without Dallas, she'd be easy picking for the killer on her trail. She tried to turn her mind to her dreams for the café and her personal life, thinking again about finding a husband and having kids. Even if Dallas got her safely to the trial, should she take the risk? Maybe it was better to plan on being lonely. She'd never forgive herself if today's choices resulted in her future family becoming a target.

Dallas climbed into the driver's seat and an image of what his children might look like flashed through her mind. They had black hair, bright dark eyes and big bold smiles. It was strangely comforting to imagine him as a father, surrounded by love and laughter. She had no idea what kind of future he had planned, but somehow it helped to believe the dreams she needed to let go might be fulfilled in his life.

"Killing me discourages others," she said after they got back on the road. "Whether or not I testify."

"They aren't good people," Dallas said. "Big operation leaders rarely go down easy. They're greedy, addicted to the money and power. Exposing three witnesses at once takes serious money and reach."

"Maybe they got a discount since the three of us were all in the area preparing for trial."

Dallas's shoulders stiffened. "You saw the other witnesses in Helena?"

"No. I just assumed based on conversations."

His chin dropped in surprise. "Conversations. Be very sure, Marnie. Did you assume, or did you hear something specific from someone specific?"

She paused, thinking through the last few days. "They moved me to a safe house in Helena three days ago. Jerry had been with my security detail from the beginning, he coordinated everyone." She appreciated Dallas's patience as she rewound the recent events. "It was over the radio, the day before yesterday," she recalled. "I overheard an exchange between a new woman on the team and someone else. She mentioned witness prep appointments. I didn't hear her give any specific times. No names either," she added. "So how would that help?"

"What was her name?"

"Amy Stillman."

He handed her his cell phone. "Text that name to Tyler. He'll follow through."

She did as he asked, setting his phone back in the console when she was done. For a long time Dallas was quiet, his focus on the road interrupted only by his cycle of mirror checks. A muscle jumped in his jaw and every few minutes, he shifted and stretched his leg.

"Where are we going?" she asked when they were well away from the boundaries of the national forest.

Another deep breath, another stretch of his leg. "While I wait for Tyler to dig up something helpful, I thought we should gear-up for a few days in the wilderness."

"Weren't we supposed to meet Hank in Eagle Rock?"

"We might still do that. Just not today."

She started to ask why and decided she'd rather not have more gruesome possibilities to consider. The bad guys knew she had strong ties to Eagle Rock. "So we're going camping."

"Pretty much." Dallas smiled. "The spot I have in mind will be close enough to Helena, assuming the trial stays on schedule. Bonus is that it's not tied to you in any way."

She thought of the bald man who'd broken into the motel room. "Won't the killer just wait for us to return to the courthouse?"

"That would certainly require the least amount of effort," he admitted.

"Great." Guilt was her own personal storm cloud on this sunny day. Being a sitting duck was bad enough. Who wanted to dwell on dying at the hands of an excellent, unknown marksman? But the idea of Dallas suffering the same fate as Jerry and never seeing those kids she envisioned for him made it all worse.

"Relax." He reached across the cab and patted her hand. "After what happened yesterday, the U.S. Attorney's office will post a watch on the rooftops and any potential sniper nests. They'll take better protective measures in transport with all of you."

She covered one hand with the other, pressing the warmth of his touch into her skin. "How will we know about the trial?"

"Tyler will keep us in the loop."

There didn't seem to be anything to do but go along with his plan. He was the expert in personal protection and she found herself trusting him more with every hour. "Thanks for coming up with a plan."

"It's a start." Dallas checked his mirrors again, scanned the horizon. They seemed to be the only car on this section of highway. "I'll feel a whole lot better when the killer is found and his intel source cut off."

CHAPTER 5

DALLAS WAS in the bodyguard business for several reasons. He'd needed a job, a purpose, after his military career ended so abruptly. Standing in the gap to protect others was apparently hardwired into his DNA. He'd been opposing bullies since grade school. But during imminent-danger cases like Marnie's, he understood exactly why Gamble and Swan had recruited him so aggressively for the Guardian Agency.

Although most of his cases weren't as intense or high-profile as this one, his thorough understanding of law enforcement and choke points within the justice system often helped him and Tyler sort things out swiftly.

He admired Marnie's conviction and courage and he wouldn't let her down. For the first time since signing on with the agency, he was questioning his protective ability. Maybe he hadn't given the cultural connection enough weight after all. Regardless, this felt bigger and far more sinister than anything he'd faced before. He couldn't immediately recall another case where three key witnesses had gone missing in the same twenty-four hour window.

Going off-grid would give them some time to regroup. With a little breathing room, he was sure he could figure out how to get her safely back to Helena. Assuming he could trust the team that would protect her at that point.

Knowing someone close to the case had leaked information about the witness locations and schedules, Dallas was half-tempted to lay out some juicy bait and set a trap. That would require backup, something in short supply out here in the middle of Montana. On top of that, he couldn't be sure Baldy was the only killer on their trail or how he was connected. Was he a hired assassin working solely for the payout or someone with a more personal commitment to the crime ring?

This case wasn't about rival drug gangs, or a dealer who'd gotten dinged in a territory takeover. Native American girls and women were being trafficked by a well-funded criminal organization. Would the people at the head of that snake trust a hired gun with something as delicate as eliminating witnesses?

As much as he didn't want to distress her, to sort this out, he needed as much information as possible.

"Do you remember how many shots you heard at the courthouse yesterday?" he asked.

She didn't reply right away. He glanced over and found her nibbling on her full lower lip. He'd be happy to take over *that* task. Damn, the sight stirred him. He had to get his mind back on the legal side of this assignment and keep it there.

Marnie tempted him at every turn. Whether she held him at gunpoint, was trying to run, or sobbing on his shoulder, he wanted more. He wanted to uncover and understand every challenging inch of her. When she'd wept in his arms, he'd wanted to kiss away her heartache, distract her from the terrifying thoughts that had so completely overwhelmed her.

There would be justice. The Guardian Agency wasn't a vigilante group, but unjust outcomes weren't tolerated. Going solely off his own cases, he and the other protectors rarely worked the standard, 'keep the paparazzi away' bodyguard roles. The agency took on unique clients and situations that often looked hopeless at first glance.

By design, he didn't have personal contact with the other bodyguards on the agency payroll, but word got around about significant successes.

"Two," Marnie said, her response yanking him from his thoughts. "One caught Jerry's arm and the second one hit him square in the chest."

"And this morning, you thought the shooter was aiming for me."

"That's right." She twisted in the seat, her full attention on him. "Do you think I'm right?"

"I'm just thinking," he cautioned. What did anyone gain by removing her protection and making her run? If the man at the hotel was different from the sniper near the courthouse, that explained a different tactic.

"This doesn't add up," she said, echoing his thoughts. "Why kill Jerry and let me go? He's no threat to the defendants."

"An interruption, a misfire," Dallas suggested. "A dozen things might have gone wrong."

Her shoulders sagged. "You're right."

"Were you close to Jerry?" Just asking the question rankled. He didn't want to think of her with another man. Outrageous. She wasn't *his*, she was his responsibility.

"He headed up my team from day one," she said.

"Were you close?"

"He was married, two kids," she said, bristling now. "If you're asking if I was sleeping with him, the answer's *no*. I'm not a homewrecker."

Great, he'd insulted her. "I was asking, but not judging." He had to shake this infatuation before he really messed this up. The client, a U.S. Attorney, was counting on the agency's superb reputation.

"Right." She folded her arms and turned to watch the scenery pass by her window.

He drove on, the rugged beauty of the area nearly lost on him while his mind was tangled with her, the situation, and the factors that didn't add up. On a better day, he'd appreciate the deep green of trees on the ridge, the wide open spaces under that endless sky. If he'd been alone, he would've rolled down the windows and followed the sounds and scents to a quiet field or an overlook where he could enjoy some solitude. In those isolated moment, he felt free to release bits of the crushed dreams that were locked in the back of his mind and heart.

He let out the pieces of pain in small doses. Though he couldn't carry the heavy grief forever, opening himself too wide, digging up too much at one time sent him into a downward spiral that was damned hard to escape. He didn't need a certified shrink to direct the process, just more time. What happened to his K9 partner was simply another example of life's general unfairness. The devastating toll of rage and sorrow was familiar. He looked forward to the day when he was truly free, but rushing the journey only resulted in setbacks.

"Why didn't Six like you?"

He shifted in his seat, organizing his thoughts. "Six didn't like anyone after being sent back to the States. No one could handle that dog until Joe showed up. From what I heard, they almost denied Joe's adoption request, but Six finally cooperated with him."

"That's sad," she murmured.

"It has a happy ending." Unlike his own K9 partnership.

Dallas had never managed to stay detached from his cases or his partners, human or canine. He'd been cautioned against early burnout, urged to maintain a wall between his individual values and the scenes he was called to. As an MP, he answered calls that ranged from awkward to outright criminal. When he'd joined the K-9 unit, the calls had often been drug related.

Yet even on his last call, he'd seen a person rather than a nameless drug-dealing perp. And he'd paid a dreadful price for his worldview. Still, he clung to that belief, continued to lean hard on that wispy faith in humanity. If the people behind the misdeeds and crimes were interchangeable, if they didn't matter, then neither did he.

He'd trained hard and been absolutely committed to making a positive and lasting difference for the people he served. He'd been determined to be more than a nameless uniform trying to keep the peace.

Dallas rubbed his palm on his jeans, wiping off the memory of his dog's blood on that God-forsaken night two years ago.

"Are you all right?"

"Of course." He glanced at Marnie. She was a woman who meant something to her friends and family. A woman who'd put herself on the line to save a young woman who'd been stolen, enslaved, and abused.

"Really? You keep rubbing your leg."

"Oh." With deliberate motions, he put both hands on the steering wheel. Ten and two, just like a brand new driver. "It's the injury." It wasn't really a lie. "The nerves gripe once in a while." Weren't memories a type of nerve and emotions another facet of pain? Same old song, new achy verse.

"Anything I can do to help?"

He bit back an inappropriate response. "It'll loosen up once we're out of the car for a bit."

"Where exactly are we going?"

"The Blackfeet Reservation," he replied. "I know it's been a drive, but we're almost there." He planned to stop at a general store and stock up for at least a week of camping comfortably. He had cash stowed in a lockbox under the seat, enough to cover the basics. Tyler could arrange for him to have more cash, but that meant heading into a more populated area and he didn't want to risk being spotted by another closed circuit camera system or caught by a cell phone.

"What's wrong? Haven't you been wondering what breed I am?"

She jerked as if he'd slapped her. "That's... that's a rude phrase."

"You're right." He couldn't make himself apologize though. Too often he'd heard people, even people who *liked* him, muttering about his upbringing, traditions and culture and how those factors affected his ability and commitment to a job. As if a straight nose, darker skin and straight black hair were outward manifestations of a learning disability. He'd heard it all, let most of it roll off, if only because that was how his grandmother raised him.

She'd fought to keep him with her on the reservation. It hadn't been a posh life, but it had been more stable than many kids in his situation. The tribal police who'd told his grandmother her daughter was dead and the county sheriff who promised to bring his father to justice had supported her petition.

His grandmother's firm guidance and open mind had empowered him to grow up with confidence in his tribal lineage as well as in the world at large. Learning what his mother had endured as an abused wife inspired him to join the Army as an MP. To help others and build a life that honored his memories of her.

He'd done it, despite the challenges. Being Native American put one more hurdle between him and every goal, but he'd succeeded with pride, his grandmother's voice in his ear every step of the way.

She'd be scolding him now for assuming the worst of Marnie. If he didn't treat his heritage with respect, why would anyone else? He straightened his shoulders. "Forgive me, please. I'm edgy because I don't know exactly who or what we're dealing with."

"That makes two of us," she said. "I wish I could do more to help."

"You're not used to being a bystander are you?" he asked.

"Not a bit." She blessed him with a warm smile.

"More gets done when people are willing to get involved."

Luck or intuition, he thought Autumn Curley had chosen the right place to make her escape attempt. "You're right." He was involved with Marnie now and an innate awareness warned him this case, this woman, would linger long after the case was closed.

"Do you have a plan?" she asked, worry at the edges of her voice.

"Nothing complicated. We'll pick up supplies and get out of sight, lay low until Tyler gives the all clear."

"Oh." She sank down in the seat, her hands squeezed between her legs.

"Am I missing something?"

"It's just that…according to Autumn, the reservations have turned into hunting grounds for Tribal Pride and the mob."

The statement slammed through him. He kept on top of crime news and trends and he'd heard about increasing action of gangs and organized crimes in and around the reservations. To learn those gangs were deliberately targeting and kidnapping their own young women was an outrage. What the hell?

"Dallas?"

His blood turned hot in his veins and his skin itched. "I'm thinking." There was probably some legal logic for why the U.S. Attorney kept that disturbing detail out of the news ahead of the trial. No one wanted to stir up racial tension or cause a community panic. "The media said Autumn was from Shelby."

"She told me they'd taken her right off the Blackfeet reservation."

He swore under his breath. "All right." He gripped the steering wheel. Odds of going unnoticed at a store on the reservation were still better than stopping anywhere else. "All right," he repeated. "My primary goal is to keep you out of sight until the trial. Can you call Tyler? Please."

She picked up his phone. "No signal."

"There's a silver lining," he murmured.

"What do you mean?" She studied the phone, and tried the call again.

"If we can't get a cell signal, it's unlikely anyone else can." Though he kept it to himself, he figured the gang hunting her would never expect her to show up on the reservation where they were operating. Having grown up here, he knew the area well. "I haven't seen another car behind us for a few miles now. Do you trust me?"

"Do I have a choice?" she countered. "Yes," she added a moment later. "I trust you."

Everything that had coiled tight inside him loosened. "Let's stick with the plan. I'd rather return to the forest closer to Helena if you can handle the return drive."

"Whatever you think is best," she said. "You're the expert."

Her flash of courage had dimmed again. She was increasingly frightened and he didn't blame her. He was the expert and he needed to stay in that professional zone rather than get distracted by her distress. She was in trouble, had been shot at three times in two days. Once her case closed, he could meet up with a woman that wasn't being targeted by the mob and put Marnie and all the impossible things she made him long for behind him.

Scared or not, she demonstrated a desire to be involved. He had to give her more of an explanation if he wanted to keep her invested in his plan to keep her safe. "I'm sticking, not because I'm stubborn or we've spent hours on the road," he began.

"It's fine."

Clearly, it wasn't. "From what you've said, we might learn something out here."

"Like what?"

"Maybe nothing," he admitted. "And maybe..." He didn't want to verbalize the foul theory brewing in his head. "Maybe we'll find out if there's a network of some sort on the reservation," he said at last.

The idea of the tribes exploiting their own made him sick, but he couldn't ignore the glaring signs. Dallas was as well-versed in Native American history as he was current crime trends. It hollowed him out to think that in this day and age, their numbers dwindling and culture fading, they still couldn't work together.

"People suck," he blurted.

Whether the root motivation was power or greed

or a warped value structure, people from every background were capable of committing violence. He'd seen it firsthand. The gangs and mob out here were notoriously ruthless, but buying and selling people was an unforgivable evil. Dallas was more than a little intimidated that the crime rings had the funds, reach and savvy to breach witness security and hire at least one killer to wreck the case against them.

The bald man he'd fought at the motel hadn't struck him as Native American. Those first, vague impressions weren't definitive, but it reinforced his worry that the gangs had hired professionals to clean up the mess. He had to tell Tyler at the first opportunity.

"I know bad things happen," Marnie said. "To everyone. When Jerry... when he went down, I was numb. Frozen."

"Shock," he said. "Completely normal." He glanced over, wishing he could say something that would make it better. He supposed the best thing he could do was listen.

"Then, it was survival," she said. "It hit me all at one that I wasn't ready to die. Especially not a statistic."

He flexed his hands on the steering wheel to keep them away from her.

"By the time that man found me at the motel, I was full of vengeance. To get even for Jerry. For Autumn. For justice in general." She laughed without humor. "I'd convinced myself I could singlehandedly take down the two men on trial and their entire mob."

"Your testimony will go a long way when we get you into that courtroom." A challenge he'd tackle when the time came.

She shook her head. "Will it matter? Someone else will just step in and take the promotion."

The defeat in her voice cracked the wall his instructors and commanders had insisted he build up. "And someone else will stand up to them, thanks to your example."

"You sound so sure."

"I've seen the ripple effect in action as an MP. One person says no to a bully of any kind and others get brave. Believe me, this case is making headlines and the attempt on your life will only add to your credibility rather than undermine the prosecution as intended."

"I really hope you're right."

"If Hamilton was truly intimidated or worried about the odds in court, she wouldn't have sent me." It sounded harsh, and he wished like hell he'd mastered tactful conversation.

"That helps." She sat up in the seat, her smile soft, but there. "Thanks, Dallas."

It was his turn to hope he was right. Whatever kept her going, kept her believing, would make the days ahead easier for both of them.

RAISED between Helena and boarding school in Portland, Oregon, Marnie had never spent much time on the reservations. When she did enter protected land, it was a matter of driving through for camping or the occasional girl's weekend at one of the casinos.

The open spaces always struck her first. The panoramic views were rugged and gorgeous and the stark differences usually refreshed her spirit. Not today. Today she was twitchy and felt watched even though they were the only vehicle on the road. Never in her life had she felt so plain and insignificant as she did now, entering the Blackfeet Reservation with the handsome, magnetic man beside her.

Her bodyguard, charged with protecting her until the trial.

She couldn't put more on him than that, not even in her imagination. Ditching him wouldn't work and she wasn't sure she'd survive if she did. She'd always relied on herself, her ability to take care of whatever curve balls life through her way. This situation eroded her self-confidence and her innate belief that it would all work out.

She'd gone her entire life in a bubble of self-assurance that if she made smart choices and worked hard she'd be just fine. Yesterday's events cracked those pillars of her life. Any minute they'd crumble and she'd be a puddle of tears and uselessness. Again.

She peeked at Dallas. He'd proven himself inventive, capable, and up to the task. Relying on him wasn't just her only move, it was the smart move. Still. They were on the same land where awful, cruel men had kidnapped Autumn and who-knew how many other young women.

"Hey." Dallas touched her shoulder. "Are you sick?"

She hadn't realized her body had followed her fearful thoughts. She was curled in on herself, as far as the seatbelt allowed, her arms clasped around her sides. "No. Just… I'm just…"

"You're safe. Focus on that. Focus on me. I'm here, you're safe."

He could've been speaking to a cornered dog or a spooked horse. And suddenly she understood why that particular tone was so effective.

"I've always gone my own way," she managed. "Stood on my own." She looked out the window at the vast rural beauty surrounding them and felt smaller than a single blade of the wild grasses bowing to the breeze. For some reason that view combined with his voice eased the knot in her stomach. "There's never been any doubt I could get through to my goals. But this situation, being under attack, is bizarre. I don't mean to keep freaking out on you."

"You aren't the first and you won't be the last," he assured her. "No one should be subjected to this kind of danger. We'll get you through it."

And then what, she wondered. "Do you think they'll keep coming? When it's over, I mean." The thought of being on guard for the rest of her days was daunting. Exhausting.

"Why bother after the fact? Once you testify, the two men on trial and the gangs in general will have bigger problems."

"You don't think I'll have to look over my shoulder for the rest of my days?"

"No."

She wanted to believe him and made a conscious decision to borrow from his confidence. Expecting trouble in the future wouldn't make today's challenges any easier.

"All right." He pulled to a stop at sparkling-clean gas station. "We've made it."

The store set back from the gas pumps sprawled out in a single story and the windows were filled with signs for sales on camping and fishing gear. "I'll fill up the tank and then we'll go stock up," Dallas continued.

She waited, reading every window ad repeatedly while he pumped the gas, expecting bullets to find them any second now.

He climbed back into the truck and moved to a parking space in front of the store. "If anyone asks, we've been dating a few months and we're headed out on our first camping trip."

"What?" She couldn't have heard him correctly. He wanted her to play the role of his girlfriend out here? That couldn't possibly improve matters, but she managed not to argue.

"If anyone is scouting for you we should know fairly quickly."

"Then what?" she wondered aloud.

He gave her a cocky grin, his eyebrows arching over his sunglasses. "Then I handle it."

"Do bullets bounce off you?"

The grin faded as fast as it had appeared. "No."

"Were you shot? Is that what happened to your leg?"

He left the truck on an indistinct grumble.

Oh, man, she'd said the wrong thing. She scrambled to catch up with him, her fingers fumbling on the door handle as worry clamped around her throat. He couldn't mean to leave her behind where a blonde woman stood out like an albino deer. She struggled to calm down, her breathing ragged when she looked up to see his face on the other side of the window.

He'd come around to open her door. "Easy," he said in that gentle tone.

The lines around his mouth were set and she wished she could see his eyes. As if he'd read her mind, he removed his sunglasses and hooked them in the collar of his shirt. "You can say anything to me. You can even try and run again. I will *not* abandon my post."

"I-I'm sorry."

He tilted his head. "For what?"

"For being nosy." She looked into his nearly-black eyes, framed by thick eyelashes and straight eyebrows. "For saying the wrong thing."

"Curiosity isn't a curse. Yes, I was shot in the line of duty. The leg is often moody and most of the time I'm not." He paused, taking a deep breath. "The short version is the shooting wrecked me, inside and out. Working for the Guardian Agency is... well it's my second chance." He looked up to the sky before his gaze captured hers once more. "Calling the job my salvation wouldn't be overstating things. I'll tell you the whole story later, if you're interested."

Oh, she was interested. Every conversation intensified her fascination with Dallas exponentially. She couldn't blame it all on proximity or fear, though those aspects were certainly factors.

He offered his hand to help her out of the truck and her palm sizzled against his. Her curiosity about him wasn't completely academic. She'd been in an extended dry spell even before getting tangled up in the trafficking case. Dating or simply hooking up while in protective custody was impossible and she'd soothed her craving for romance and intimacy through books and movies.

He slipped an arm around her as they walked into the store and a rush of heat and hopeful hormones flooded her system. She was probably transferring that long-running loneliness to Dallas. All things considered, that wasn't an outrageous reaction. He'd saved her life twice over. She might be resourceful and stubborn, but she recognized she was in over her head against the person so willing to kill her.

"I just want to go home," she murmured.

"Ah, don't say that." He led her toward the clothing

section. "We'll turn this trip around, sweetheart." His lips brushed the top of her head.

She looked up, startled, and then remembered the plan. They were supposed to be dating. Smiling, she rubbed his arm, enjoying the play of muscles under his shirt. "You're the best."

"I am," he teased. "Start with a warmer jacket," he suggested. "The nights will be cold."

"Right." His real girlfriend wouldn't have to worry about being cold with Dallas close. The man radiated heat and strength.

"Make sure you grab whatever you'll be comfortable in for hiking." His palm slid across her back and he pulled her into a quick squeeze. "I can't believe we forgot to load up your pack."

The contact felt so natural and familiar she didn't have to pretend to enjoy it. Maybe Dallas wouldn't mind ending her dry spell once they were somewhere safe tonight.

"Hey?" He murmured her name low enough they wouldn't be overheard. "You okay?"

She pressed her lips together, swamped with too many conflicting emotions. Shoving her hands into her pockets, she tried to smile. "I'm good. Overwhelmed." That was pure honesty. "I should've made a list."

His smile was beautiful, indulgent, as he pulled an item off the rack behind her. "Try this on."

She turned, slipping her arms into the sleeves of the coat he held. The thin layer of soft fleece inside would be a big improvement over her denim jacket and the rain and wind-proof outer shell was perfect for the weather this time of year.

"The hood is zipped into the collar." His thumbs stroked over the nape of her neck and out across her shoulders as he spoke. "Want me to open the zipper?"

Oh, yes, please. She caught herself before she melted under his hands. Scooting out of his reach, she tested her range of motion. She had no business thinking about zippers of any variety, in coat collars or other places.

This had to be some weird emotional reaction that psychiatrists published papers about. Fear and stress exacerbated by her sexual dry spell. Being attracted to a ripped, smart, and confident man was also natural. She'd been in distress, Dallas had come to her aid and now they were sorting out the case. None of it was a big deal, aside from the bullets, and those weren't flying right now.

He was here to keep her alive so she could testify next week. End of story. He didn't need her coming on to him because she couldn't keep her stress hormones in check.

"Feels good." She fiddled with the pockets and snaps that covered the zipper, keeping her eyes off the man she was ready to jump. They definitely didn't need to draw *that* kind of attention.

"Looks good on you."

His voice teased her senses. She would've sworn

he'd touched her again, but he was standing in front of her, hands in his pockets, watching her intently. He tilted his head. "You shop and I'll get the food. Trust me to remember your favorites?"

She nodded. He was the type to notice the little details that would make his girlfriend feel special. Sure it was his obvious skill and commitment to his job, but part of it was just him. And she did trust him, this man who was little more than a stranger. He'd won her over somewhere between the campground bathhouse and opening her door.

"Just give me five minutes," she said at last. "I know we want to get to the campsite."

"Take all the time you need. It isn't that far."

He sounded like everything she'd ever wanted in a real boyfriend. Patient, kind, affectionate. Marnie shook off the delusion. Sexy, she added, ogling his butt when he walked toward the grocery side of the store.

"Need help finding anything?"

Marnie jumped at the query and felt her face heat up at getting caught staring. "Yes, please, Hanna," she said, reading the young woman's nametag. "I need a pair of jeans and a couple of shirts. The essentials and boots too, if you have them. We managed to leave my gear back at the apartment.

Hanna rolled her eyes. "Let me guess, you were in a hurry?"

Marnie chuckled. "You could say that." In her estimation, Hanna was hovering right around twenty. Her glossy black hair was braided over her head like a headband, leaving her fresh, pretty face unframed. Her dark eyes twinkled conspiratorially. "Your boyfriend's hot."

"I think so."

"Have you been together long?"

"Not too long, no," Marnie answered without thinking. "It's our first big trip. Camping seemed like the best next step," she joked.

"Good luck with that." Hanna tilted her head. "You look really familiar."

Through a spike of fear, Marnie managed a chuckle. "I get that a lot. I must have one of those faces."

With a shrug, Hanna turned her attention to the stacks of denim, quickly finding Marnie's size in the style and cut she preferred. "You should try these on."

"I'm sure they're fine. I know he wants to get on the road."

Hanna leaned close and bobbed her eyebrows. "I saw the way he looks at you. He won't mind waiting a few minutes."

On that cryptic comment, Marnie was ushered into a dressing room with two pairs of jeans. A moment later, three shirts were flipped over the top of the door with tank tops and long sleeved shirts for layering.

Marnie wriggled into the new clothes, impressed by the girl's talent for judging her size and preferences. Being in something clean, despite the same bra and panties made a world of difference.

She didn't want to lean too heavily on Dallas's expense account, so she chose items she knew she'd wear after this was over. Stepping out of the dressing room, she found him waiting right beside her door. "I didn't expect you to be right here." Her heart kicked at the heat in his eyes when his gaze skimmed over her.

"We need to hustle." He shoved a pair of boots at her, brand new socks stuffed inside one of them. "Try these on."

"Okay." His urgency clear, she sat down on the bench and made quick work of changing out of her flats. Tugging the socks over her feet, she quickly laced the boots. Designed for comfort, the new boots supported and cushioned her feet just like a great pair of sneakers. She stood, bouncing a little and rocking back and forth.

"They're perfect," she said, stepping out of the dressing room again.

"Good."

His smile was too tense to be of much comfort. "Did they find us?" she whispered as he escorted her to the register. He wasn't hovering, he was practically smothering her. She'd had more room to breathe when he rushed her out of the motel. Or maybe it had only felt that way.

"How did everything fit?" Hanna asked, beaming at her. Her smile turned flirty when she looked at Dallas. "You seem to approve."

"It's all great, thanks." He was tearing at price tags and handing them across the counter.

"Happy to help."

"I could've changed back into my clothes."

"Oh, this happens all the time. We're used to it." Hanna stated the total and Dallas handed over cash to cover the bill. He seemed increasingly agitated as Hannah carefully folded each item.

"Oh. That's it," she exclaimed, sliding the full shopping bag across the counter. "You're the woman from Eagle Rock. You rescued—"

Dallas slid his arm around her waist, guiding her toward the entrance. "Thanks for your help. We need to get rolling."

Hanna rushed around the end of the long counter. "Hang on, I just wanted to say thank you."

With an effort, Marnie slowed Dallas's momentum. "I didn't do anything. Not really."

"But you did," Hanna insisted. She reached out and pulled Marnie into a hug.

For a moment, with Dallas still holding her hand, she felt like a hank of rope at the mercy of opposing forces.

Hanna released her. "You helped *so* much. Most of the time no one *does* anything but talk. You're a hero." She looked up at Dallas. "You must be so proud to know her."

"I am."

Marnie blinked at the sincerity in his voice and the admiration stamped on his serious face.

"She's an amazing woman," he added, shocking her further. "But we do need to get going." He handed Hanna a business card. "You were a big help to us today. If we can ever return the favor, reach out."

"What favor can we return?" She struggled to keep pace with his ground-eating strides as they left the store. Whatever problem he had with his leg, it didn't seem to be an issue right now.

"You never know." He pressed the button on his key fob and the doors unlocked. He practically shoved her inside along with the shopping bags and groceries.

She barely got her butt in the seat before he slammed the door closed.

He stopped so suddenly, she gawked at him. Something in the distance captured his full attention. Something unpleasant and behind them, based on the angle of his face and the slight curl in his lip.

Slowly she twisted in her seat, braced for the worst. All she could see was a small dust cloud in the distance and the glare as sunlight bounced off the windshield of a vehicle.

From this distance and in this area, she guessed compact pickup truck. And based on the way the vehicle bounced over the uneven road, the driver was speeding.

Dallas motioned for her to get down. His lips moved, but if he'd spoken the order as well, she didn't hear it for the sudden buzzing in her ears. She obeyed, though she was tired of hiding. Every time she did nothing to help herself she felt as if she'd never take positive action again.

The unwelcome awareness had set in with the official move to protective custody and grown worse with every day that separated her from the life she'd built. She had zero regrets for helping a brave girl break free of her captors. She just wanted to be sure she didn't get lost in the justice process.

Tucked under the dash again, she vowed to find a way to reclaim the pro-active woman she'd been.

CHAPTER 6

DALLAS ALLOWED that he might well be edging toward paranoid. Having security experience, he'd noticed the cameras around the store right away. Maybe they should've left immediately, supplies be damned. The whole point of shopping here had been to stay *off* the radar, away from cameras that could be accessed by anyone and away from people who might recognize Marnie from the news reports.

With his background, he shouldn't be making these dumb mistakes.

Sure he'd wanted to learn if the gangs had issued a criminal equivalent of an all-points bulletin for her. Dumb move. If that truck bearing down on them was connected to the gangs that were snatching girls off the reservation and he'd effectively dropped her into their laps, he might be sick.

Well, he'd be sick later, when he had the luxury of

time and she wasn't in danger.

It was too late to get away cleanly. Leaving in a mad rush would bring down all kinds of unwanted attention. If these new arrivals weren't random, they knew Marnie was with him and what kind of vehicle they were in.

Hope fired through him when the truck rolled to a stop at the other end of the parking lot. The typical gang move would've been to block him in. Two men emerged from the cab of the rusty pickup, both average build and height and wearing dark T-shirts and worn jeans. At first glance they looked like a normal couple of ranch workers stopping in to grab a six-pack or fill up with gas.

Dallas wasn't quite ready to believe his eyes. He pretended to scrape something from his front fender and casually moved toward the driver's side of his truck.

The driver pushed his hat up a bit and asked Dallas about fishing in the area. When Dallas didn't respond, the driver added a slur about 'natives' that Dallas ignored. He'd learned early on that jumping into fights over words wasn't the best use of his time or his talents.

"I asked you a question!" The driver barked.

Dallas turned toward the driver, fully aware that the man's friend was circling around to the back of his truck.

"Look at this, Max," the friend said. "Guess the

native boys don't use tee-pees anymore."

"That so?" The man named Max stepped closer to Dallas. "How'd you get money for all this? You the chief's top brave or something?"

Dallas had to do something before they saw Marnie. Whether or not these idiots were with the crime ring, it would be difficult explaining a white woman shoved under his dashboard. He was being baited, definitely, but were they just hapless jerks or part of the gang with more sinister intentions?

"Have a nice day, guys." He moved toward the driver's side despite Max standing in his way, drawing their attention. "There's a camp site waiting on me."

"You saying you got a right to this land?" Max snarled, clearly spoiling for a fight. "You ain't got no authority over me."

Dallas shook his head. "Federal government settled all that generations before you or me." He wanted to get the hell out of here without more trouble. Any movement now all but guaranteed both men would be close enough to spot Marnie.

Max folded his arms over his chest. "Eli, this native boy needs a lesson in manners."

Dallas held his ground as Eli rushed him from behind. As nice as it would be to have an assist from the Tribal Police, he couldn't risk that intervention exposing Marnie.

He let the man tackle him to the ground, let him think he had the upper hand. At his pal's encouragement, Eli landed a couple good, hard knees into his kidneys and rubbed Dallas's face in the dirt. When he let up long enough to gloat, Dallas made his move. Not quite as quick as he'd been before the shooting, he was fast enough to gain the advantage over a swaggering bully like Eli.

He had Eli pinned in a few seconds. Max bellowed and charged and Dallas braced for the blow. It didn't come. The other man shrieked in pain and lurched to the side.

Marnie was there, holding a knife stained with Max's blood. "Come on!" she shouted. "Hanna's probably called the police by now."

Dallas cuffed Eli on the back of his head, hard enough to daze him before following her order. He started the engine and shoved the gearshift to Reverse, flooring the gas pedal.

"What the hell, Marnie?" he demanded as they left the store behind.

"It's not a serious wound. I know how to use a knife," she said, her nose in the air. "A few stitches and some aloe for his burned pride will fix him right up."

"I had it under control," he insisted.

"Did you?" She looked around the cab and finally dropped the knife to the floor. "You were on the ground and Max was ready to pile on."

"I was fine." He checked his rearview mirror as he turned onto the main road. But he didn't head south for the national forest near Helena. He turned north toward the mountains. "When we get a signal again, call Tyler."

"Sure. And you're welcome."

Adrenaline held him in a fierce grip right between his shoulder blades. One more incident and he'd take her to his grandmother's place. No cell service, no paper trail and no ties to her history. Maybe that's what he should do right now. As soon as he was sure they hadn't been followed he'd decide.

He tapped the button on the steering wheel to call Tyler, even though he'd asked her to take care of it. He needed a touchstone about now, some normal aspect of working a case to smooth out the jitters. Still no signal.

Mile by mile, he pulled himself together and took stock. She was safe. That had been a skirmish with a couple of bigots, that's all. He'd had worse fights with friends during his Army days. They had food and she had the right gear for a few nights in the wilderness. Thanks to Hannah, they knew Marnie's face had been on the news, but he'd expected that. They were low on weapons. Or so he'd thought. He glanced at Marnie and noticed the smug pride on her face.

"You're remarkable," he said, cursing the tremor in his voice.

She rocked forward in the seat, her hands gripping her knees, before she eased back and looked at him. "We're clear?"

He checked the mirrors again. "Looks like it."

"Where are we going?"

"Up into the mountains. At least for tonight, if you won't mind the cold."

"Yesterday I was braced to lay low without any gear. Now I'm all outfitted, including a warm coat. How can I be anything but fine?"

Remarkable, he thought again. "You're still at the top of the mob's hit list. That might put a pinch in 'fine' status."

"I have you for that," she said sweetly. She powered down her window, the breeze teasing her long, pale hair.

He wanted her to have him, for whatever suited her. Clearing his throat, he tried to drag his mind back to proper ground. "You handle yourself," he said. "I'm sorry I barked at you."

"Apology accepted."

"Feel better?"

She slid him a sly look. "I do actually. Hiding is *not* in my nature. I know I need your help, but being useful goes a long way to quashing the persistent fear."

"Barring a dirty play or a sneak attack, my money's on you in a one-on-one fight."

She arched an eyebrow and twined her blowing hair around her hand. "How about you keep your money and we just avoid more attacks?"

"Works for me," he admitted.

He let her drift in her thoughts while he drove up into the mountains on the less-traveled roads. Unless a tree was down, he knew where he could safely go off-road without breaking laws or getting caught. His destination tonight was a beautiful spot near a waterfall that would give them plenty of privacy and fresh water as well excellent views and a second egress if they were found.

On the way, he stopped near a park ranger station just long enough to get a text message out to Tyler before they lost the cell signal again. Confident Tyler could handle the research, Dallas drove on up to the intended campsite.

As he'd hoped, the area was clear. He and Marnie were completely alone and far enough from the marked trails to stay that way. He cut the engine and opened his door, just resting a minute and breathing in the mountain air.

The sound of the nearby waterfall made him smile, easing the last of the tension from his shoulders after the past twenty-four hours. There was nothing quite as healing to him as this particular slice of the wilderness. It had been one of the challenges of moving away from the reservation to the Army. He didn't regret his original career plan, but it was one more perk of his fresh start as a bodyguard.

"My God, Dallas." Marnie hopped down out of the truck and turned a slow circle. "This is absolutely gorgeous."

"You grew up in Montana, you know how beautiful it is."

"Well, yeah. But places like this…" Her voice trailed

off and she leaned back against the side of the truck, her face tipped up to the sky. "They just steal your breath."

He'd never shared this particular location with anyone. Never wanted to, but it had been second nature to bring Marnie here.

Watching her take it all in was a nearly-erotic experience. Her hair blowing in the wind, her lips parted, breasts rising on a deep inhale. He wanted to gather all that hair, pale as sunlight, into his hands and nuzzle that supple curve of neck to shoulder. What scents lingered on her skin right there?

He turned away from the view of her and thought about the cold water in the falls nearby. A dunk might be necessary to get through the night without crossing a line. "Curious about the real view?" he asked.

"Definitely."

Her eager gaze cruised over his chest and his stomach dropped. No use blaming adrenaline. Better to suck it up and admit he was attracted to her. More than that really. His body didn't give a damn that she was a client and therefore off limits. For the first time since the physical therapy released him, his practice of ignoring his body's random outbursts came in handy.

Wanting her couldn't be helped, but acting on that desire was completely within his control. He gazed up to the sky, soaking up every soothing aspect of the area. Sunlight danced over the towering pines and unmovable rocks, testifying to the permanence of nature. People were fragile and brief by comparison. Here, he'd always felt utterly removed from any angst or trouble. He didn't bring her here for a seduction. He would share this restorative gift with Marnie without mucking it up with a wayward erection.

They chatted about camping experiences while they set up the tent and inflated the air mattress. Marnie secured their food against raccoons and bears and Dallas implemented a few precautions in case they were found. When he was confident they'd done all they could, he guided her around to the waterfall.

Conversation became impossible as they neared the rush of water pouring over the rocky cliff. He took his time, carefully creating a path for her and offering a steadying hand. He suspected she didn't need the assist, but he felt ten feet tall when she rested her smaller hand in his. Taking this route gave his leg a welcome challenge and the screaming nerve gave him a respite from the way Marnie affected him.

When they finally reached the main path and the rarely visited official overlook, the wide smile and bright joy on her face was worth every discomfort. He slowly paced the ache out of his hip while she marveled at the beautiful pocket of serenity.

"I wish I had a camera."

"Promise not to post anything online?" He didn't think the cell signal would be strong enough out here, but he'd rather be clear than make an assumption that could expose their location.

She nodded, eagerly accepting his offered phone and turning toward the falls. Eventually, he settled on one of the park-installed benches while she *ooh-ed* and *ahh-ed* and took what must have been a thousand pictures. It was a refreshingly normal interlude. Comfortable and friendly, feelings he hadn't enjoyed often enough since leaving the Army.

"What are you thinking about?" Marnie asked, taking a seat at the opposite end of the park bench he was lounging on.

Her gaze was on the powerful beauty of the waterfall and he took advantage of the moment to study her profile. The soft line of her cheekbone, delicate curve of her ear on down to the firm set of her jaw. He'd never in his life ruminated about a woman's ear, but he could spend hours tracing that gentle shell up and around and back down to her neck.

He couldn't confess any of those thoughts. "I needed this reminder that the world had good spaces and good people."

"That's what I like best about my café in Eagle Rock."

"Not the food?" Every attempt to keep his thoughts on professional ground was failing. Not that she needed to know that.

"Well, I do love feeding people," she admitted. "And complaints about the food are few and far between, so I guess I'll just stop trying to be modest and say I do like the food we serve. Edie and I created a fabulous menu."

He laughed. "Own it," he encouraged. He silently vowed that one day he'd get to sit at a table and watch her work. "Takes guts and courage to be successful in business. Especially the food business."

She rolled her shoulders, as if the compliment was hard to accept. "We're taking the long way around it, but my favorite part about my café is seeing good people. Happy people. Not everyone is a delight every day," she allowed.

The day she'd helped Autumn escape couldn't have been much fun.

"In general though," she continued. "I like where I landed and I love what I do."

"That's really important." He'd felt that kind of pride and contentment of purpose as an MP. Until his K9 partner had been killed, leaving him floundering in a well of grief.

"I imagine you don't see the best of people in your line of work."

"As a bodyguard I protect good people," he said.

"But you protect them during times of stress. I can't be the first client to batter you with a lousy attitude. Or a flood of tears."

"Stress does twist up the nicest person," he agreed. Grief and stress and wondering about how to rebuild his life had twisted him up for months until the Guardian Agency had brought him on board.

"So how often do you bring your clients here?"

He chuckled. It sounded like some cheesy line from

one of the black and white movies his grandmother had adored. "You're the first. I usually stick closer to the client's primary location."

"What do you mean?"

"The agency has regional operators. When I was hired, they told me I had to be ready to answer a call immediately. I don't think I've ever been more than two hours from getting the protect order to being on duty."

"Sounds intense."

"It can be." Until Marnie, the intensity had always been reserved for the case itself. This increasing yearning, this draw for her specifically, was completely new.

The light was fading and they really should get back to the truck before full dark. Standing he turned and held out his hand. "We should head back."

She put her hand in his and stood. Alarm bells sounded in his head. He'd miscalculated. The hot zing of her skin sent his longing screaming into full-blown need. In the fiery glow of the sunset, her skin was gilded, her lips pure temptation.

He shouldn't move. Couldn't. He told himself to step back. His feet didn't budge. Her fingers rested in his palm and time slowed as her tongue slipped across her lips. Those pretty blue eyes held him captive in a sensual net as she closed the distance and pressed her mouth to his.

The sweet, almost-innocent contact shook the solid rock under his feet. He slid a hand around her waist, up her spine, holding her close. If he was going down, he'd damn well do it the right way.

MARNIE SIGHED, her body softening, molding to the hard planes of Dallas. All of his considerable strength, firmly planted to the earth, kept her tethered while the kiss sent her flying.

She was kissing her bodyguard. Kissing him in front of the prettiest waterfall she'd ever seen. The moment was a study in glorious perfection with the sun setting the sky ablaze with beauty. She felt daring and free, with his tantalizing taste and scent rising around her, enveloping her. His embrace a solid and sure reminder that here, with him, she was safe.

His lips cruised over her cheek, along her jaw. She couldn't quite catch her breath. His mouth returned to hers and she didn't care about breathing. He eased back, tucking her head to his chest and she heard his heart pounding under her ear.

It was a comfort to know she wasn't the only one affected.

Without a word, he guided her back around the waterfall. At least he hadn't called the kiss a mistake or anything. Need rocketing through her, it was all she could do not to stumble the whole way, just so he'd keep touching her. Craziness.

She'd been kissed. She'd initiated kisses. But kissing

Dallas eclipsed her prior experiences and made her long for more. More than she had a right to ask, but she couldn't stop hoping.

He was here as her bodyguard and she was pretty sure the job description didn't include sexual favors. Maybe it *was* the job, his role as her protector from the bad guys that appealed. Or maybe, she mentally crossed her fingers, it was a real connection.

A connection strong enough for two consenting adults to explore in the moment. Would he go for that? The conversation played out in her head.

Hey, Dallas, we could die tomorrow. Let's enjoy tonight.

I won't let you die, Marnie.

Good to know, but why not err on the side of caution?

There didn't have to be a future. She didn't need any promises. Considering who was hunting her tomorrow wasn't guaranteed. Inwardly, she cringed. Less than twenty-four hours ago she'd worried about putting him in a killer's sights. What kind of person was she that today she'd toss aside her concerns in the name of potential pleasure? A person who'd been too long in a sexual desert faced with a sexy, irresistible oasis.

In reality, going further than kisses would be the polar opposite of caution. But now that the possibilities—the images of his body tangled with hers—were in her head, she couldn't shake it off. Didn't want to. Was his skin that gorgeous, sun-kissed color all over? Would he give her free rein or take charge?

She wanted to explore both options, all of the options.

She did stumble, thanks to her wandering thoughts, and went down hard on her hands and knee. Look at that, a true Freudian slip. She laughed at her own joke, despite the sharp sting in her palms.

"Are you all right?"

"I'm fine," she responded, popping to her feet. But her knee locked and she pitched to the side, ruining her bravado.

Dallas caught her. Of course.

"Fine, huh?"

"Fine enough." She ran her hands up his biceps to his shoulders, unable to resist the temptation. "My knee just needs a minute."

Holding her steady in one arm, he used his free hand to tip her palm to the fading light. His thumb soothed as he gently wiped away bits of dirt and debris. "We'll clean you up and then we can eat."

She wanted to gobble him up in one quick bite. Or savor him for hours. Just as long as there were more kisses. More everything.

He must have caught the heat in her eyes. His entire body tightened a fraction and her belly quivered in anticipation of another kiss. Instead, in a lightning-quick move, he scooped her into his arms. She could only hang on, breathless, as he carried her to the campsite.

At the truck, he set her gingerly on the tailgate. "Wait here."

She nodded, too afraid if she tried to talk she'd babble like a giddy teenager. She heard him rummaging around in the cab of the truck. A moment later, he returned with a bottle of water and what appeared to be a first aid kit.

"Were you a Boy Scout?" she mused.

He looked up from cleaning her palms, one eyebrow raised. "I was independent until the Army," he replied. "Hang on."

He leaned past her, his hip pressing against her thigh. She bit her lip to keep from moaning. A light came on and he clipped it to a hook on the tent pole overhead.

"Independent or not, you could teach survival stuff," she observed.

His hands were gentle as he washed her scrapes and rubbed ointment into the deeper scratches. Still, her mind wandered through the myriad ways those hands might touch the rest of her body. She had it bad and if she didn't get this under control, she'd jump him soon.

"Thanks," she murmured as he packed up the first aid supplies. "Tell me where things are and I can take care of dinner."

"I've got it."

"All right." She looked around the area. Remote or not, she wasn't sure she wanted to risk a fire. "Do you have a camp stove?"

"Yes. And I'll take care of it. Just relax, Marnie."

Not a chance. How could she relax when he was close enough to touch? They were tucked away in a forest, surrounded by the sounds and scents of nature, yet *he* overwhelmed her senses. His body was as rugged and sturdy as the terrain and more enticing that the surrounding woods.

"Why are you so calm?" she demanded.

He stopped working on the meal and stared at her, apparently speechless. Her abrupt question seemed to be the only thing in the last hour or so that rattled him.

"This is my favorite place."

And she was the only person he'd brought here. Did that mean something? "Your favorite place in this park."

He shook his head slowly, his gaze locked on her. "It's my favorite place. Period. No qualifiers. In all that I've seen of the world, nothing beats it." He stirred the canned stew heating on the stove and then pointed up to the sky. "Nothing beats that view. Day or night."

She disagreed. Not even the gorgeous array of stars twinkling overhead could compete with the man in front of her. She'd never been this hung up on a man.

"You do," she whispered.

He winced.

Had she misread his reaction to that kiss? He hadn't rejected her, why did he seem so reluctant to be near her now? Please let it be something like professional pride and not an outright personal rejection.

"Should I apologize for kissing you?" She wouldn't, but it seemed like the right question.

"No."

"Is there someone else?"

"No," he repeated.

"Then what's the problem? Did I offend you?"

"No."

"Dallas," she warned, her temper rising. "Find more words." She saw his mouth twitch, recognized he was fighting against a smile or joke or some kind of snarky comment.

Easing down off the tailgate, she joined him at the camp stove.

"Careful," he said.

"I don't want to be careful, Dallas. I want you."

The spoon clattered and it seemed the rest of the world held its breath, along with her, waiting for his response.

"You shouldn't, Marnie. You can do better."

She huffed impatiently. "I'm going to need more than that. And don't try and tell me this is some protector-infatuation thing."

"Isn't it?"

"No. I've been in protective custody for six months waiting on this case to come to trial."

"Did anyone try to kill you? Did anyone have to rescue you?"

The questions made her think, but they didn't make her doubt what she was feeling for the man in front of her. "No. There were threats and I had to be moved once, but—"

"What? You were moved?" he interrupted. "No one put that in the record. Tyler would've told me if he'd known."

Despite the desire pounding in her bloodstream, his reaction gave her pause, diverted her attention. "Why is that a problem? Jerry told me that it happens sometimes."

"Rarely." He surged to his feet and paced away from the little stove. "Was that before or after Amy Stillman got involved in your detail?"

"I didn't see her until the house in Helena," she answered. "But that doesn't mean much. There were spotters on the team that I never saw personally. Maybe she was only new to me."

"Right. Right," he muttered, pushing a hand through his hair.

She picked up the spoon, tending to the food he'd forgotten. The stew simmered and her stomach rumbled. Dallas retreated to the truck. When he returned, she divided the food between two bowls and handed him one when he paced within reach.

Turning off the valve on the small propane tank, she watched him. "You should sit down to eat."

"In a minute." He shoveled a bite of stew into his mouth. "You were only moved once?"

"Yes."

He grunted and downed another bite. Looking

around, it took him a moment to spot the water he'd brought out earlier. Picking it up, he finally settled beside her.

As dinner dates went, this one ranked fairly high on her scale. Her companion might be quiet, but he wasn't making awkward small talk and the atmosphere and view couldn't be beat.

Comparing this dinner with Dallas into the context of meals with her personal security, it was at the top of her chart. She enjoyed the expressions moving across his handsome face as he worked through whatever troubled him. The man's formidable nature was tempered by compassion and of course it was no hardship to simply be in the vicinity of his sex-appeal.

"Do you plan to share what's on your mind or should I just call it a night?" she asked. She didn't want to give up, but it seemed that delicious ribbon of sexual tension had been shredded by his distraction.

She could hardly fault him for being consumed with keeping her alive.

Disappointment was unreasonable. The man had been hired to protect her and he was doing a fine job, her infatuation notwithstanding.

"The move should've been in your file. I went back and checked, but it's not there. Even if I'd overlooked it initially, Tyler would've caught it."

"Why does it worry you?"

"This is only an educated guess, but your location must have been leaked *before* yesterday's fiasco."

Leaked, as in someone purposely exposing her. Well, sure. She'd come to the same general conclusion, even before telling Dallas about the exchange she'd overheard. The who and why seemed irrelevant, interchangeable, since the real source had to be the gangs calling the shots within the kidnapping ring.

"They wouldn't have moved you unless the threats were immediate and verifiable."

"You…" Her voice failed. She cleared her throat and tried again. "You're saying someone came close to killing me months ago."

He reached over and chafed her suddenly cold hands. "Yes."

She flinched, even knowing how he'd answer. They moved her because the mob found her and sent in a killer to silence her. A killer who'd taken out a man she considered a friend. A killer who'd tracked her deep into a national forest, determined to succeed. She understood why the men who'd lost control of their 'property' didn't want Marnie to testify, but she had no idea their bosses could get to her behind legal protection.

"Can you recall the names of the first responders who reached the café?" Dallas asked. "What about the first FBI agents you spoke with? Who else interviewed you? The leak has to be fairly high up the food chain," he added. "Either someone with a lot to lose or someone with a lot of leverage."

She heard him and she wanted to help, to give him a

name or detail that would bring this nightmare to an end. Looking up, the stars took a slow spin overhead as the terrifying situation robbed her breath, made her heart race.

"Easy, Marnie." His voice sounded so far away. "Hey, now. Stay with me."

She couldn't quite cooperate. When she could focus on his voice again, she found herself in Dallas's embrace again. One warm palm smoothed her hair back from her face his face was close to hers. He was singing softly, a lullaby she didn't recognize.

"What happened?" She tried to sit up, but he didn't let her.

"Give it another minute."

Another minute? "What happened?" she asked again.

"You fainted a little." His lips feathered against her forehead.

"No." That wasn't her. Wasn't possible. Fainting was a weak-girl thing and against a killer a weak girl was toast. "No," she repeated. "Let me up."

He supported her and she wanted to curse him for it. But it was nice to have his chest at her back, his legs bracketing hers. "I don't faint."

"My fault," he said, unmoving. "I was peppering you with questions. I'm usually better than this."

Facing away from him, the area lit by the glow of the lantern at the tent, she felt braver. About some things anyway. "Why aren't you better at this right now?"

She felt a deep breath move through him. She wanted to believe she was special, to him in particular, beyond the scope of a client.

For most of her life she'd hoped to become special to someone. Her parents loved her, but always from a distance. Their careers had frequently taken them on the road and they'd seemed content to leave her with nannies as needed. Having given her every educational opportunity, they'd been confounded by her decision to tie herself down to one small restaurant in what they considered a nowhere town.

In Marnie's mind that small-town factor was the best part. She'd been sinking roots in Eagle Rock from day one. Making friends and gathering regulars who'd felt like family. She'd worked to hone her interests into skills and build her skill into a viable business. On purpose or not, she'd created a way for people to feed her craving for appreciation, while feeding them as well. It seemed a strange time for an epiphany. Then again, the life and death consequences should inspire some introspection.

Being in protective custody, she'd been lost. She cooked for the team as often as possible, baked and played with new recipe ideas, but it hadn't been the same thing. The case threatened her identity. Not just her name, but how she viewed the woman she'd become. She wasn't sure she could hit reset and start over as a brand new person. Who would she be if she wasn't Marnie Kemper, owner of 'that cute café' in Eagle Rock?

"You get under my skin," Dallas said quietly, interrupting her thoughts. "That kiss."

A ragged breath pressed against her back, subsided. "I'm a professional," he muttered. "Supposed to be anyway."

She assumed the words were meant to remind both of them of the expected boundaries. "You are. You've proven your expertise a few times over." Daring to try again, she covered his knee with her hand. "Thank you."

He tensed, but didn't move away from her touch.

"If we'd met like normal people, do you think I'd still get under your skin?" She was pushing him, but she needed to know. Everything around them seemed to go still, waiting for his answer.

"How do normal people meet?" he quipped.

She wanted to be mad, but the amusement in his voice sent a bolt of heat through her system. "Usually an app," she replied in kind. "I've watched more than a few coffee-dates in the café."

"I've never been on a coffee-date," he said.

Of course he hadn't. "You probably just walk into the grocery store and women fall into your cart. Beg you to take them home."

Laughter, low as distant thunder rumbled through him. "Well, sure," he said. "It's easier than any app."

She squirmed around to face him. This was so

much better than talking about what might become of her, about the threat that sent them out here. "All right. Here I am, Dallas. I've fallen—thrown myself—into your grocery cart. What's your move, Mr. Bodyguard?"

He tilted his head. "Is this before or after you've begged me to take you home?"

He acted as if the idea of a woman throwing herself at him was absurd. Wasn't she proof to the contrary? Leaning in, she rested her palms on his thighs. The long, firm muscles were taut under his jeans. Her mouth watered as a wealth of delectable, sensual possibilities flooded her imagination. She was done with appropriate roles, over the distraction of bad guys and killers. They were safe out here tonight, it might be the last safe night she had for a while.

She licked her lips, watched his dark eyes track the movement. "Take me home with you, Dallas. Pretty please."

He slid a hand over her cheek, into her hair and pulled her mouth to his. She'd barely registered the pleasure when he stretched out on the ground keeping her with him, over him, while his mouth fused with hers.

All of him under her gave her a jolt of awareness as life-altering as a lightning strike. Her nipples peaked against his hard planes of chest and she gave in and rubbed against him like a cat, pressing her body into his. "Yes," she murmured against his skin, her mouth skimming along his jaw, down his throat. She'd never have enough of the salty, woodsy flavor that was only him.

He sat up, pulling her thighs wide over his legs and the hollow ache at her core made her moan. This man could soothe that ache, fill her completely, body and soul. "Dallas," she groaned as he cupped her breasts in his hands, teasing the sensitive tips.

She wriggled closer until she could rock against his erection. He groaned and pushed her shirt up and off. He swore once and pulled her close enough to tease her breasts through the thin fabric of her bra. She arched and cried out, holding his head close, already on the verge of an orgasm.

She couldn't interpret his response. The gruff words rumbling across her heated flesh sounded like praise and his breath sent goose bumps racing over her skin. There were far too many barriers between them. She scrambled to pull his shirt over his head and out of the way. Her first view of his chest made her whimper. There was ink, from shoulder down to his wrist on his left arm. It was too dark to make out the finer details, but she traced the lines she could see until her fingers laced with his. She brought his hand to her lips, kissed his fingertips, his palm while he watched her.

"You're beautiful," she breathed.

He closed his eyes tight, shook his head. The resistance to praise only made her more determined. They both moaned as she smoothed her hands over the warm expanse of sculpted lines and angles of his torso.

His abs were a fantasy. He rolled back, letting her indulge and explore. Good man. This moment under the stars was a step out of time, they might be the only two people in the world.

Kissing him all over, she followed the ridges of definition down to his waistband. He moved restlessly beneath her as she unbuckled his belt so, so, slowly. It was a sweet torture, filling all of her senses with him, wallowing in the anticipation.

Until he stilled her hands. "Marnie, wait."

She nearly growled. Or screamed a denial. She'd thought they were on the same page here. "Why?" she asked with precise calm.

He brought her face close, bumped his nose to hers. "This isn't my normal MO. I need you to understand that. I've never wanted a client like I want you."

She relaxed. He wasn't calling it off. "I get it." She did. "I do. Truly." She caressed the hard line of his shoulders. "Neither of us can control how we met."

"Seems neither of us can control our attraction," he agreed.

"Do you want to?" Suddenly nervous, she wished she could withdraw the question.

"Not even a little. I just…" He kissed her again. "It doesn't change anything. My job is to keep you alive, safe, so you can testify."

"You're great at your job, but please let me live a little, with you." She feathered kisses over his striking face. "Here, tonight. I will beg."

He chuckled and brought her mouth back to his. Thankfully, there was no more talking. Only sheer, glorious pleasure as they stripped away the last of their clothing, baring each other to the moment and the night sky. He left her just long enough to grab a blanket from the tent to protect them from the rough ground. His body was a work of art, painted with tattoos, shadows and secrets and the odd scar or two.

No man had tempted her this way or made her feel so worshipped. The way he caressed her with his hands and mouth was everything she'd deemed impossible. He drove her to a fast orgasm with his hand, his fingers deft and quick through her slick folds. She'd barely caught her breath before he had her writhing beneath his mouth, begging for another release.

He prowled over her limp body, pausing long enough to roll a condom over his erection. Next time, she promised herself, next time she'd get a taste of him first.

Then he was at her entrance, thrusting deep. They fit together so perfectly. He filled her senses inside and out. She rose to meet him, taking him deep and deeper still. She stroked his arms and shoulders, wrapped her legs around his lean hips and held on, held him. Overwhelmed, she let him take her over the blissful edge one more time. When he shuddered, a low growl buried in the curve of her neck, she smiled up at the stars.

CHAPTER 7

DALLAS COULDN'T BELIEVE he was bare-ass naked outside, buried balls-deep in a client. Except that wasn't fair to either of them. She was so much more to him than a protect order. And she was right. They couldn't help how they'd met. If this woman had jumped him at the grocery store he hoped like hell he'd have had the sense to take her straight home.

She was heaven in his arms, supple and eager, with a passion that stoked his. Making love with her here added one more reason to the long list of why this was his favorite place on the planet.

He wanted to give her sweet words and all sorts of promises he shouldn't make. Not while she was in danger, not before she testified. He nuzzled the curve of her neck, breathing in her soft scent and then left her just long enough to deal with the condom properly.

The air cooled his sweaty skin, but he didn't want

to dress, didn't want any barriers between them. Not tonight. For tonight he wanted to pretend nothing else mattered, that nothing could ever interfere with this stunning happiness.

These whirling thoughts and feelings in the aftermath of amazing sex and what he wanted from the future might be impossible. He'd keep her alive, no matter the cost. But after the trial... it was too soon to know what her life would look like then. Would the mob persist in hunting her out of vengeance and make an example of her?

With a leak somewhere in the judicial system, would she ever be safe?

Yes! A voice in his head shouted that he could keep her safe always. He was such a cliché, wanting to stake a claim and keep her forever now that he'd had her under him.

He hit the pump to inflate the air mattress and then returned to the blanket and the woman he wanted again already. She reached out a pale hand. He bent, kissing her fingertips, loving the contrast of her skin next to his.

Kneeling, he wrapped the blanket around her to keep her warm. Gathering their clothing, he carried it to the safety of the tent. It wasn't as if they had much and he wasn't inclined to risk another supply run should a raccoon or the elements take a shot at their limited wardrobe.

She was dozing when he came back for her and

adorable with her muffled protests.

"You'll thank me in the morning," he said. Wrapped in the blanket, he carried her to the truck and urged her into the tent. He extinguished the lantern and crawled in beside her. Stretched out, he pulled her close to his body, chuckling when she yelped.

"You're cold," she grumbled.

Beside her, he'd warm up fast enough. "Not for long." He explored her body in the dark, lingering over every dip and curve, savoring each variation in the taste of her skin from her nape to her shoulder to belly and lower still. Her arousal tempted him as he sucked and nibbled on her inner thigh, working his way to her core. He was relentlessly patient, until her hips were bucking under his mouth, her hands tangled in his hair as she gasped his name.

Marnie at the height of pleasure was a sight as beautiful as a sunrise and one he'd cherish forever, no matter what tomorrow threw at them.

A few hours later, Dallas woke with the sun. He crept out of the tent and pulled on his jeans, then walked out of sight into the trees to deal with life's necessities.

Marnie was still asleep when he returned. Having worked up an appetite, he started on breakfast. Regretfully, he'd opted for stocking prepackaged foods rather than stocking up on fresh ingredients that made a camping breakfast special.

Uncertain if he was more amused or annoyed with

this new drive to impress her, he put water on for coffee. He heard her rustling around in the tent and was about to see about lending a hand when he heard his cell phone.

He hadn't expected a signal strong enough for a phone call out here. Darting to the cab, he answered the call from Tyler. "News?"

"Not any you'll like," his assistant said. "I had to root through the equivalent of a Dumpster before I found anything helpful."

Dallas noticed the tent had stopped moving. Marnie was listening.

"I'll probably lose my job for this," Tyler continued, "but when I was looking for connections, I found that the firm that handles our company business, has a connection to U.S. Attorney Hamilton in Helena."

"We're a word of mouth operation, Tyler. Since when does a friendly connection surprise you?"

Tyler snorted. "Hamilton and Gamble were married in law school."

"Oh." Dallas whistled. "That's, ah, interesting. I won't breathe a word." He caught Marnie staring at him through the window of the tent. Wishing he could simply kiss away the frown pinching her brow, he winked. She blushed.

"What about the garbage, Ty?" he asked, getting back on track. He needed information not gossip.

"She was moved due to threats against her. The documentation was almost successfully trashed.

Someone got close enough to rough up one of the outside guards. Hamilton removed herself from the email chain shortly after the relocation was approved. I can't even find out where they moved her, only the last address in Helena is in the file, though I've verified that safe house hasn't been in use since Marnie's team vacated the premises."

"You think the leak is in the U.S. Attorney's office?"

"I do, but I haven't tied it to Stillman. I'm searching bank records for signs of payoffs now."

"Keep it up," Dallas encouraged.

"Don't I always?

Dallas heard Tyler's hands working on his keyboard. "Is there more?"

"Yes," Tyler said. "If I'm on speaker, pick up."

Dallas did as he asked. "What is it?"

"Our agency has been assigned to find the other witnesses on this case," he said. "Do *not* ask me how I found out. Autumn Curley inexplicably escaped her security detail. Those reports read as if she disappeared into thin air. The woman who saw the two bastards on trial kidnap her sister was attacked when her detail tried to move her."

Shit. Hamilton's slam-dunk case was falling apart. "Well, if there's one thing the mob didn't count on it was the Guardian Agency," Dallas said.

"Damn straight."

"Any suggestions for how to get this killer off Marnie's tail?" he asked.

"You're the guy in the field," Tyler said. "But there is some good news on that front."

"I'm listening."

"After combing through everything I'm pretty sure you're dealing with just one man."

That *was* good news. "The bald guy?"

"That's the one. I've shared everything I found through CCTV with Hamilton's office. I might be tipping off the bad guys too, but it had to be done."

"Nice job." Dallas said. "Thanks."

"I'll keep on it. You two should stay out of sight until the trial."

Dallas's eyes caught Marnie's. Hiding out with her would be a pleasure. But he wondered how long he could manage it. She wasn't the type to sit back and wait and she was still carrying buckets of misery and guilt over the man who'd died protecting her. "Is Hamilton asking for a continuance?"

"Not sure," Tyler answered. "I'll keep you posted."

"We'll do the same."

"Yay." Tyler didn't sound the least bit enthused, but he ended the call before Dallas could say anything else.

For the next few days, he and Marnie filled their days with long hikes and conversations that ran the gamut from holiday traditions to favorite ice cream flavors. Every sweet kiss was better than the last, every night in her arms a new discovery. He was already crazy about her, though he didn't trust his feelings enough to share.

It wouldn't be fair to put it out there while he was still so integral to her ongoing safety.

She seemed content with the arrangement, adopting a vacation frame of mind, but she went quiet during Tyler's update calls. His assistant found a likely payoff in Stillman's bank records, but he couldn't locate the source. Reporting it to Gamble and Swan, they had to trust the agency attorneys to inform Hamilton.

Unfortunately, finding that money trail didn't expose the killer who was probably still searching for Marnie in order to cash in.

Day by day Dallas's desire to stay with her increased, yet he couldn't help wondering what she'd do when she was truly free again. He wanted to believe they were building something real, but worried he was only deluding himself.

They'd hiked up to the ridge with a picnic to watch the sun set. Tomorrow they'd have to make a supply run and the logistics were weighing on him. If he had his way, he'd leave her here, hidden, but she'd never agree to that.

She linked her hand with his as a blaze of indigo stretched across the sky. "What was your partner's name?"

The question was so unexpected, he answered without thinking. "Reggie." To his further shock, speaking his dog's name didn't scald his throat. "I haven't spoken his name since the memorial." One more miracle courtesy of Marnie.

"There was a memorial?" she asked.

He nodded. "Once I was out of the hospital."

"I'm sorry, Dallas."

He looked up at the sunset and thought of his partner. "He knew it was going sideways before I did." He swore, pinched the bridge of his nose. "I tried to defuse the situation, but the perp was done, determined to go out in a wild gunfight. Reggie died at the scene, covering me after I went down."

She reached up, wiping a tear from his cheek.

Without any effort, all of the details spilled out of him. He told her everything about meeting, training and working with Reggie. He shared the quirks of his Belgian Malinois who had a nose for drugs, a goofy side, and a heart of pure gold.

She was still holding him, kissing the tears from his cheeks when the cell phone chimed with a text. "Tyler's perfect timing," he muttered. Clearing his throat, he held the phone so they could both read the message.

News. Your bald friend is lurking in Helena. Authorities on alert.

"He's clearly planning to make his move when you to testify," Dallas said. *Or after.* He looked up and saw the same resignation in Marnie's blue gaze. "I won't let him through."

"What if we did?"

Dallas reared back. "Pardon me?"

"What if you take me back to Eagle Rock and we

just…" She pushed at her hair. "What if we draw him to us there?"

He had to take a long slow breath. This wasn't the time to lose his cool. "Using the spunky female as bait is a Hollywood move. This is your life we're talking about. I don't want to take chances with you."

"You think I'm spunky?"

He rolled his eyes. "I think you're a lot of things. Sexy. Spunky." He gripped her hips and drew her into his body. "Did I mention sexy?"

"Never hurts to say it again."

"Beautiful." He kissed her, leaned back. "My first thought, seeing you in person, was that you have the prettiest eyes I've ever seen."

He boosted her up and she wrapped her arms and legs around him, sinking into the kiss. When he set her back on her feet, she swayed just a little and giggled, but he knew he hadn't changed her mind.

"Go on and tell me how it's working in your head," he said.

He listened attentively, making suggestions and recommendations. By the time they reached the campsite, they had a plan that didn't leave him in a cold sweat and didn't put her at too much risk.

MARNIE COULDN'T BELIEVE she was actually in her bedroom. *Her* bedroom in *her* house in the town she'd made her own. Sure the curtains were drawn, but that was temporary. As soon as Dallas caught Baldy, she could throw the windows open again and let in the light, literally and figuratively.

She paced the width of her bedroom as she wrapped up her call with Edie, then handed the phone back to Dallas. "Thanks for that."

"Get everything sorted out?"

"She's already spreading the word."

Sprawled across her bed, naked, he smiled up at her. Her heart did a happy spin in her chest. She'd never get tired of being on the receiving end of such sincere affection. Growing up, her parents had reserved their happiest smiles for the newest customer or most recently closed deal. The sliver of resentment felt strange and a little awkward. Those days were long gone. This time with Dallas had done that for her, reminding her she was her own woman. She'd forged her own career in a place that felt more like home than any of the houses she'd grown up in.

She felt her lips curling in response to him. "I told her we're sticking close to the house to keep trouble away from the café, but I really should go into town long enough to replace my cell phone."

"I don't mind sharing."

Of course he wouldn't. He was Mr. Generosity with his time, his stories, and his miracle-inducing body. Was it because she was a short-term deal or did he care about her? She supposed she'd find out soon. Once

Baldy made his move, Dallas would catch him. Then everyone would get back to life as normal.

Suddenly life without Dallas didn't feel like the normal she wanted.

She turned away from him before she said something she couldn't retract. Being an expert observer, odds were good he already knew she'd fallen in love with him. She wished she had some way of guessing his feelings for her. It felt like one more serious disadvantage to have to be the first to say the words.

And what a confession that would be. She could hear it now, it sounded too much like a pop song in her head. *I know we just met and this is crazy, but I'm in love with you and I want to have your babies.*

She would've laughed at the absurdity of her altered lyrics, if they weren't so accurate.

A few days ago, she'd imagined how beautiful his children would be. Now she was envisioning a more specific scene, one in which they stood hand in hand, watching *their* children play. Sometimes there was even a dog in the yard. Not a working partner, but a treasured companion. Oh, she was silly.

He'd probably been stepping over love-struck women for most of his life. She didn't want to be part of the pile and she didn't know how to ask if she was different without sounding pitiful.

"You remember what to do when he attacks?" Dallas asked.

"Yes." She slipped into her robe and went to the

kitchen corner and put the teakettle on the stove to heat. "I call Joe and then run toward town." Both Hank Patterson and the sheriff had men posted all around Eagle Rock, ready to support Dallas and subdue the killer.

He came up behind her, wearing only his boxers, and wrapped his arms around her waist. "That's right. Whatever you hear, keep running."

She nodded, though it was the one promise she might have to break. "With any luck, one of the others will nab him before he gets in range of." He kissed her cheek, tucked her hair behind her ear.

"Do you do *this* to all your clients?"

He pulled back immediately, his gaze shuttered. "What do you mean?"

She hadn't meant to offend him. Stepping closer, she brought his warm hands to her hips. "Bore them to death with memorization exercises." She stroked the excellent cut of his arms as he relaxed. His tattoos fascinated her no matter how long she studied them. "Death by any means can't be good for business."

His fingers dug into her hips and then he boosted her onto the countertop and kissed her. His tongue stroked across hers and she melted. That simple, delicious contact was all he needed to have her ready for him.

She gripped his shoulders for balance now as desire swirled around them, pulled them out of the crisis until he was the entirety of her world. Here in his arms it didn't matter how they met or how long ago. This raw, glorious connection was all that mattered. She'd rather focus on Dallas for all the time they had left than worry over what other people considered standard relationship patterns.

She wound her arms around his neck and her legs around his lean hips. He gripped her butt and pulled her closer, grinding her center against his arousal.

"I need you, Dallas," she confessed against his lips. Desire blotted out everything but him. She loved the way she was with him. For so long she'd had to rely solely on herself. But she trusted him to keep his word. Whether they were planning evasive maneuvers or sexual pleasure, she could count on him. With every piece of her body and heart.

She'd never held back with him and wouldn't start now. The freedom in that choice made her feel beautiful, empowered, as his hands skimmed over her, stripping away her robe. He bent his head to her breast and she arched into the gentle nip, the soothing stroke of his tongue.

Working his boxers down over his hips, she wrapped her hand around his erection. Stroking him base to tip, he shuddered, dropping his head to her shoulder with a ragged groan. She reveled in his responses, loving that she could give him the same bone-deep pleasure he showered on her. He kicked his underwear aside, then grabbed her hips and carried her back to the bed.

She laughed, pretending to wriggle away, letting him drag her back. He froze, staring at her. "Dallas?" If Baldy attacked now, she'd kill the man with her bare hands, to hell with the plans to capture him alive.

"You deserve lace and silk." His eyes were dark with passion, his muscles popping.

"Do you have a thing for lingerie?"

"I guess so." He shook his head, as if he couldn't quite clear his vision. "You in lace might kill me."

"Challenge accepted." It underscored her hope to think of a future shopping expedition for lace that would stop Dallas's heart.

He nipped at her hipbone, making her giggle, before settling between her legs with a sexy growl. He lapped at her slick folds and she was lost to the sparkling sensations in a heartbeat. He played her body so expertly with his fingers, tongue and teeth. He teased, she begged. He pushed her to the edge and kept her there until she was mindless, craving the promised release.

"Dallas, please," she cried, hardly recognizing her voice.

"Easy, darling. Easy." He blew softly on her aching flesh and goose bumps raced across her skin. He flicked his tongue over that bundle of nerves and her body rocketed over that edge at last. He held her to his mouth, extending her pleasure until she was utterly boneless.

His kisses danced up over her belly, her breasts,

until he fused his mouth with hers. When he plunged deep into her body, the world finally seemed to right itself. She stared up into his chiseled face, touching as much of him as she could reach. He was glorious as the climax seized him, a delicious weight when he relaxed over her.

Smoothing her hand through his hair, she promised to tell him she loved him as soon as she caught her breath.

DALLAS STARED at the ceiling while Marnie dozed on his shoulder. He marveled at the twining path that had led him here. Could he even be sure of where he was? He never left himself open like this, yet he couldn't seem to keep his emotions in check with Marnie.

He couldn't bring himself to regret anything they'd shared. Marnie wasn't typical, in any sense of the word. She didn't resemble his ideal woman, other than being female and sexy as hell. He'd scrambled to draw a new line, to set a new limit that he wouldn't violate and now it was gone too. She might not know it, but he'd given her his heart. Not a piece, the whole damn thing.

He was as invested in her emotionally and spiritually as he was physically. It alternately terrified him and gave him an unprecedented sense of peace. Loving her meant her safety wasn't a matter of professional expertise and pride. Losing her now would end his career and shred his soul. In her sleep, she curled into him and he held her close, smoothing her pale hair back from her face.

How it happened didn't matter. The bigger issue was convincing her to keep him around after the immediate danger passed. For the first time since this case had begun, he wished for the next attack. Get it over with, put an end to the case so he could test out something personal.

Did he want something personal?

Hell yes. As long as that personal something was with Marnie. He was already dreading the next case and nights on the road that would take him away from her sensuous, gorgeous body.

Of course she had a life too. One that didn't include having him attached to her at the hip. He wanted that for her, wanted to see her eyes sparkle with excitement for the café and her plans for growth. Could he fit into her world? Did she even want him to?

He loved his work. She loved her work. But was there really a way they could work together?

As a Guardian Agency bodyguard, his cases were cherry-picked, the backup and resources limitless. The intense danger Dallas and Marnie had been coping with was rare. Would she believe that or would worry kill their chances for happiness? The only way to know was to ask her to give him a chance.

He hoped he was man enough to say the words when the time came.

She sighed, her breath a soft flutter across his chest, her knee sliding up his thigh. It was a clarifying moment. Marnie was all that mattered. She was it for him. Whatever she needed, he'd find a way to be that for her.

CHAPTER 8

DALLAS AND MARNIE played house for another full day without any trouble and he was wondering if he'd miscalculated Baldy's intent. He couldn't believe the mob had given up, not with the trial set to begin the day after tomorrow.

They'd just returned from the welcome home party Edie had set up at the café when the bullet plowed through the front door. Marnie hit the floor, her pretty eyes wide with fear and he knew using her as bait had been arrogant foolishness.

Footfalls hit the porch. "Stick to the plan," he said.

Trusting her, he crouched next to the door, biding his time. Baldy kicked in the door and Dallas came up with speed, under his gun hand. He knocked the gun away and put Baldy in an arm bar, ushering him back out to the porch. Baldy twisted free before Dallas dislocated his shoulder. They grappled, Baldy determined to get to Marnie and Dallas more determined to protect her.

Baldy fought ugly and Dallas took several hard blows. A knife glinted under the porch light and Dallas dodged the man's aggressive advances. He lunged, Dallas blocked, and the knife got stuck in the porch post. In his head, Dallas tracked the time. Help was coming. Joe and the others were close. Marnie had to be at least halfway to town by now.

Baldy caught him in the hip and gained an advantage, slamming Dallas over the porch rail. He hit a step, or maybe a tree, the way stars danced in front of his eyes. His were heavy as he tried to defend himself. It felt like he was fighting under water rather than the clear mountain air.

The sound of a barking dog mobilized him. That had to be Six. Dallas wouldn't let Joe or Marnie or anyone else see him failing. Baldy swore and turned for the house. Ignoring the ringing in his ears and the pain in his leg, Dallas ran after the killer.

He caught him, taking him down just before he got inside. If Baldy discovered Marnie wasn't there, he'd bolt and they'd lose him. Marnie deserved better than looking over her shoulder the rest of her life.

His hands wrapped around the man's ankle, Dallas felt the shape of another knife. He dodged the predictable kick to the face, but lost his grip. Baldy pulled the knife and dove on him.

He heard Marnie scream, figured it was his imagination until Baldy reacted. It was enough of a distraction that Dallas shoved him aside and rolled to his feet. The earth still wasn't quite steady under him, but it was a vast improvement.

Unarmed, Dallas improvised. He dodged the next attack and pulled off his shirt as they circled, each of them looking for the opening. He twisted the fabric between his hands, hoping it would hold up for a few seconds.

Marnie was safe by now and backup would arrive soon.

Dallas's reflexes were off from the tumble over the porch rail and he misjudged the angle of the next attack. The blade sliced through his side and the smell of blood filled his nostrils. Still, he moved closer, taking away the other man's advantage. He drove his elbow into Baldy's ribcage, and wrapped his twisted shirt around the hand with the blade, pulling it down with force.

The man somersaulted, losing the knife. He tried to counter when Six entered the fray, taking Baldy by the collar and dragging him down, holding him there. Breathless and unsteady, Dallas propped his hands on his knees and tried to suck in as much air as possible.

"Dallas?" Joe jogged up to get Six under control while the sheriff cuffed Baldy. "Man, are you okay?"

"Is she safe? Is Marnie with you?"

"She's safe," Joe said.

"All right." Dallas let himself fall to the ground, staring up at the deep velvet sky awash with stars.

"Dallas?" Joe asked. "Talk to me."

"I'm fine." He waved off the attention, pressing his shirt to the wound in his side. It wasn't bad. Couldn't be. Marnie was safe, so everything had to be fine. "I just need a minute."

Joe and Six sat down next to him.

They caught the killer. Alive. Marnie was finally safe. She could testify as planned, doing her part to see that two more nasty men paid for their crimes. His job was done. He wished like hell it felt more like a victory.

Did this start the countdown until they parted ways? Sure he still had to coordinate with Hank Patterson's team until she delivered her testimony. His protect order might even be extended if the gangs threated to retaliate. Doubtful, but only time would tell.

Following the trial, she'd want to get back to running her business, having a life. And he had things to do too. Work. The Guardian Agency could send him anywhere at any time. It was hardly the career that fit Marnie's ideal life.

What if—He derailed that train of thought before it could leave the station. He loved her. He just didn't know if he could give her the stability she craved. Was it fair to her to even try?

"Dallas!"

Her voice pulled him, moth to flame, and he sat up, raised an arm. "Over here."

She rushed to his side. "Are you hurt?" Her hands flitted over his face and head, down to his shoulders. God, he was going to miss her touch.

"Just catching my breath." Not an easy task when having her near made his heart race. "You were amazing." She'd been an inspiration.

"I knew you had my back." She stared at him expectantly and he locked his arms around her, buried his face in the sweet curve where her neck flowed into her shoulder. He would leave and let her live her life, just as soon as he breathed her in one last time.

"Joe is worried about you."

Dallas glanced around. When had Joe and Six left? "I'm okay, really." Dallas managed to stand up without leaning on Marnie. The nerve in his leg griped and stabbed at him, but he didn't care.

"Will you stay with me tonight?" she asked as they walked down the street toward the people gathered around emergency vehicles. "They want me to stay at the bed and breakfast since the door is busted."

Tonight. He'd take it. "Of course." He'd miss her tidy house. Once the porch and door were repaired, all it needed was a picket fence, a couple of kids and a dog in the yard. Kids with Marnie's big eyes and sweet smile. "Unless you'd rather use the tent."

Her eyes lit up, but she couldn't answer as people swarmed them. Joe pulled him aside. "You good?"

Dallas nodded once.

"I'm not talking about the leg or that gash in your side."

"It's a scratch," he countered.

"You love her," Joe said. "Have you told her?"

"Like it matters."

"It matters," Joe said sternly. "Don't be an idiot. All I wanted to say, there's room for you here in Eagle Rock, if you're interested."

He opened his mouth to reply and lights danced in front of his eyes, not all of them on the emergency vehicles. He heard Joe shout. Then Marnie. They dumped him on a stretcher and he couldn't even complain.

His mind was full of Marnie when he finally succumbed to the injuries and the meds they were pumping into him.

THEY WERE ALIVE. Both of them. Marnie clung to that fact with her heart, mind, and every fiber of her being. Dallas was too tough to die. She'd seen him perform all manner of physical feats in the past week. One nasty brawl with a killer wouldn't be the end of him. She couldn't, wouldn't, allow him to sacrifice himself for her. Not like this.

"If he dies…" She couldn't finish that sentence.

"He's alive and they'll keep him that way," Joe promised.

He'd driven her to the hospital and the sheriff had followed minutes later to take her statement. Joe spoke quietly to Hank while Six sat beside her chair. The dog let her sink her hands into his ruff and stroke his ears.

"Dallas is a good man," Joe said, returning.

"I know." She'd met plenty of people from all walks of life and Dallas would've stood out at any time. But these last days, having been hunted by the worst of men only to be saved by the best of them, made some things crystal clear.

Dallas wasn't just a good man, he was the only man she wanted. She loved him and the sooner she told him, the sooner she could start convincing him to stick around.

To her relief, a doctor emerged from the ER and explained they wanted to keep Dallas overnight for observation. It took a little convincing and a flat-out lie about being his fiancée, but they agreed to let her stay overnight in his room.

The nurse on duty let her shower and gave her a scrub top and pants so she could get rid of her torn and bloodstained clothes. She pulled the chair close to his bedside and held his hand in between the mandatory visits for the concussion protocol.

He either hadn't seen her lurking in the shadows of the room or didn't have anything to say to her. That was okay. She had enough to say for both of them. He'd stayed by her through the worst days of her life. She would stand watch for him now. Forever if he'd let her.

Near dawn, the nurse came in again and Marnie stepped out to find some coffee. She got two cups, just in case habit prevailed and Dallas woke with the sun.

The room was quiet when she returned, the lights still low. The bed was empty, but she saw him silhouetted by the window.

"You're up." A lousy observation when she wanted to cheer over him standing there, tall and proud.

"Finally," he said. "Is that coffee?"

"Fresh from the brewer in the lounge." She walked closer, suddenly shy. Uncertain. He took the cup she offered and inhaled the aromatic steam.

She soaked up every detail the low light allowed. The sunlight filtering through the blinds helped, but not enough. She wanted to move the gown aside and check the wound with her own eyes and hands.

Instead they stood there like two awkward strangers.

"Are you feeling as strong as you look?" she asked.

"Joe didn't leave you here alone?"

Their questions collided in the quiet room and they stared at each other for a long fraught moment. Until she laughed. He smiled and her heart lit up.

"Joe and Six escorted me to the hospital," she explained. "The sheriff has a deputy watching your room and the floor all night." Her fingers tingled with the need to touch him, to give and take assurance that they'd survived. She managed to keep her hands to herself. At least until he finished his coffee. She could hold out that long.

"So, mission accomplished," he said into the lengthening silence.

"Your mission, yes." She had a new mission, a new goal, and it was time to spell it out for him. The light was improving by the minute and it gave her courage, seeing the color in his face, the familiar set of his sculpted features.

"Don't tell me Hamilton is asking more of you." His voice was hard as granite, a flash of anger in his dark eyes.

"No. This is personal." She turned the coffee cup in her hands without drinking it. She was jumpy enough. It was only her heart on the line here. Her present and future happiness.

"I love you, Dallas." Saying it opened the floodgates. "That's all. You don't have to say it back. I fell for you in the bathhouse, I think." She set the coffee cup aside. "When you kept me from running away." She flapped a hand in front of her face, blinking the tears from her eyes before they could fall. She would share her feelings and face him with a clear view. "Anyway. I needed to say that. I love you. And I would love it if you stayed in Eagle Rock. With me. If your agency will let this be your home base."

He stared at her, his expression flat, only the barest

movement on his lips. Not anything as definitive or helpful as a smile or a frown.

"No obligation or pressure," she added, her confidence withering.

This wasn't a fleeting infatuation. This was the real deal. The way he'd protected her might be his job, but the way he'd touched her had been much more. She couldn't believe it was one-sided, that he didn't feel something for her.

She could *absolutely* believe that he didn't want to admit it.

"All right," she said, her words breaking the silence. "Now you know." She rocked back on her heels, inching toward the door. "I'll get out of your way. One of the deputies can probably give you a lift when you're discharged."

She opened the door, her heart breaking. She couldn't stay here waiting for him to say what she wanted to hear.

"Marnie."

She stopped in her tracks, helpless to do anything else.

He crossed the room in swift, sure strides and reached around her to close the door. His scent, under the clinical smells of the hospital, tickled her nose.

"I love you, Marnie Kemper."

Her heart stopped for one glorious second. Maybe two. And then it kicked, galloping away from her, sending a blast of heat and hope through her system.

"I needed to say that too." There was a tremor in his hand when he reached out. "I'm not going anywhere." He cradled her face in his hands, rested his forehead against hers. "I can't live without you, sweetheart."

She wrapped her fingers around his wrists, felt his pulse racing. "Good. Because I'm not too proud to say I would've followed you until you came to your senses."

His lips curved and he chuckled. It was heaven when his lips touched hers. It had only been a few hours since his last kiss, but this one meant everything to her. This was the first kiss of a happy future.

He loved her. He'd said it. He would stay right here, with her. The prospect of building a life took on a new, joyful glow.

She was home. Not just in Eagle Rock with the mountains at her back and the café up the road, but *home*. Here in the arms of the man she loved and adored, the man who could make her laugh and sigh, she would always be exactly where she belonged.

EPILOGUE

"You were wonderful," Dallas said. "My sexy, brave beauty."

Between Hank's team, Tyler's sleight of hand with computer records, and Marnie's unflappable composure, she'd made it to the courthouse in one piece. Not only that, she'd held her own under a tough cross-examination. Dallas had seen that particular brand of defeat and frustration on defense teams before.

"I think I'm still shaking," she admitted.

"No one saw anything but a strong, calm, and reliable witness."

She hugged him hard. "I wouldn't be any of those things without you."

"You were all of those things before we met." He slipped an arm around her waist, guiding her toward the exit, keeping his body between her and the windows.

There was no credible threat anymore, but he would never take any chances. She was his. A priceless treasure. And she held his heart. "I love you," he said for her ears only.

It was probably obvious to the men from Hank's team who flanked him, but he didn't see the point in broadcasting his emotions all over the place.

"You never quit, do you?"

He paused while Joe and Six checked the door and cleared a path to the waiting car.

"I'll never quit loving you," he admitted. Nothing felt as good as telling her how much he loved her.

"I meant the protector habit." Her smile lit him up like the morning light spilling over the mountains. "You think I didn't notice you've put your body between me and any threat."

"Well, I guess I'll have to be more subtle." He kissed her nose. "It's a habit you're stuck with for life, Marnie."

"Same goes, Dallas. I'll always have your back."

He felt her body brace as the door opened. "Sweetheart, that's why I sleep so well at night."

She laughed, the tension fading even as they hurried to the waiting car. It was a gift, her trust in him. A miracle and a gift he valued beyond measure.

They buckled up and she reached for his hand, weaving her fingers through his. After losing so much and having all of his plans go awry, he'd been sure satisfaction, contentment and love were out of his reach.

He'd never been so happy to be wrong.

ALSO BY REGAN BLACK

Guardian Agency - Brotherhood Protectors crossover novels

Dylan

Mike

Nathan

Unknown Identities Series

Bulletproof

Double Vision

Sandman

Death-Trap Date

Unknown Identities - Brotherhood Protectors crossover novellas:

Moving Target

Lost Signal

Off The Radar

Escape Club Heroes Series

Escape Club, prequel

Safe In His Sight

A Stranger She Can Trust

Escape Club: Justice, novella

Escape Club: Sabotage, novella

Protecting Her Secret Son

Braving The Heat

A Soldier's Honor

More Romantic Suspense

Colton Family Showdown (October 2019)

A Soldier's Honor

Colton P.I. Protector

Killer Colton Christmas

Runaway Secret

Romantic Suspense written with Debra Webb

The Hunk Next Door

Heart of a Hero

To Honor and To Protect

Her Undercover Defender

Gunning For The Groom

Heavy-Artillery Husband

Investigating Christmas

Marriage Confidential

Reluctant Hero

Knight Traveler Series, paranormal romance

Heart of Time, prequel

Timeless Vision

An Heirloom Amber, novella

Timeless Changes

The Memory Key, novella

Timeless Light

Matchmaker Series, paranormal romance

The Matchmaker's Mark

The Matchmaker's Curse

The Bodyguard's Vow

ABOUT REGAN BLACK

Regan Black, a USA Today and internationally best-selling author, writes award-winning, action-packed romances featuring kick-butt heroines and the sexy heroes who fall in love with them. Raised in the Midwest and California, she and her family and two adorably arrogant cats now reside in the South Carolina Lowcountry where the rich blend of legend, romance, and history fuels her imagination.

For early access to new book releases, exclusive prizes, and much more, subscribe to the monthly newsletter at ReganBlack.com/perks.

Keep up with Regan online:
www.ReganBlack.com
Facebook
Twitter
Instagram

facebook.com/ReganBlack.fans

twitter.com/ReganBlack

instagram.com/reganblackauthor

ORIGINAL BROTHERHOOD PROTECTORS SERIES

BY ELLE JAMES

Brotherhood Protectors Series

Montana SEAL (#1)

Bride Protector SEAL (#2)

Montana D-Force (#3)

Cowboy D-Force (#4)

Montana Ranger (#5)

Montana Dog Soldier (#6)

Montana SEAL Daddy (#7)

Montana Ranger's Wedding Vow (#8)

Montana SEAL Undercover Daddy (#9)

Cape Cod SEAL Rescue (#10)

Montana SEAL Friendly Fire (#11)

Montana SEAL's Mail-Order Bride (#12)

Montana Rescue (Sleeper SEAL)

Hot SEAL Salty Dog (SEALs in Paradise)

Brotherhood Protectors Vol 1

ABOUT ELLE JAMES

ELLE JAMES also writing as MYLA JACKSON is a *New York Times* and *USA Today* Bestselling author of books including cowboys, intrigues and paranormal adventures that keep her readers on the edges of their seats. With over eighty works in a variety of sub-genres and lengths she has published with Harlequin, Samhain, Ellora's Cave, Kensington, Cleis Press, and Avon. When she's not at her computer, she's traveling, snow skiing, boating, or riding her ATV, dreaming up new stories. Learn more about Elle James at www.elle-james.com

Website | Facebook | Twitter | GoodReads | Newsletter | BookBub | Amazon

Follow Elle!
www.ellejames.com
ellejames@ellejames.com

facebook.com/ellejamesauthor
twitter.com/ElleJamesAuthor